CANNON

CAGED AND DANGEROUS

MILLY TAIDEN

Published By
Latin Goddess Press
Winter Springs, FL 32708
http://millytaiden.com
Cannon

Cover: Jacqueline Sweet

January 2022

Created with Vellum

ABOUT THE BOOK

Breaking out of a supermax prison is nothing. Breaking away from Ryver Fernando, that's another story.

The government has me locked me up like a wild beast. They've suppressed the dragon inside me. Well, this beast is about to receive a get-out-of-jail free card and all hell is gonna break loose.

The deal is simple. Rescue a female human in exchange for my freedom. Sounds easy, right? It's not, because she's my mate.

She's the woman that makes my dragon roar. The one who gets his scales hard and boils his blood with desire.

I don't want to want her. But I can't help fate. I

don't want her smile to affect me, but it freakin' does. Perhaps we could live happily ever after, except there's one big problem.

Her mother's the one who imprisoned me.

Talk about an awkward meeting with the in-laws. This one's gonna be a war.

CANNON

CAGED AND DANGEROUS

NEW YORK TIMES and USA TODAY BESTSELLING AUTHOR

MILLY TAIDEN

— For Nydia Cabrera.

Your memory lives on.

And for my precious girl Bellita.

Te quiero de gratis.

ONE

RYVER

The sun beat down on Ryver, making her body sweat heavily, but that wasn't going to stop her from doing her due diligence. She had been sent to the Central African Republic with Adam and Luke McKay, two of the most renowned doctors from the Ivory Institute. It was an honor even to be asked to join these men, and she wasn't going to make a mockery of it. She was the only woman on the trip, and she was going to make other female doctors like her proud.

Thousands of children within the republic had been orphaned by an overarching disease that was capable of quickly penetrating the lives of those living in poverty. It was a crisis that very few within the Western world probably cared to know about. Ryver and the McKays moved from village to village giving the children medical attention and distributing vaccines as quickly as possible. They weren't exactly welcome within every region, so they had to be efficient and discreet.

As the sun dipped below the jungle canopy, Ryver sat in her hut, breathing deeply. Her anxiety had been high during the day due to armed men attacking the village they were in. The men weren't freedom fighters. They were marauders who stole what resources they needed to survive.

Focusing on the children and their medical needs, Ryver had been able to keep her blinders on until that point. Someone had alerted them, and they had to escape through a back alley, leap over a fence, and get into the vehicles or have all of their medicine and supplies taken.

Ryver breathed out hard, sitting on her cot. She thought about her dad. Perhaps her father would be satisfied by this turn of events, having to tap into the military genetics she had forgone ages ago. He had wanted her to go into the military just like him and her mother before she had died. But she couldn't leave her father for so long. If she were on her own, at least she could visit him whenever she needed.

It was late and she should try to rest. She lay down and practiced a few breathing methods that often helped when she was restless. She had just dozed off when four men stormed into the hut.

She rose from her bed, confused and dizzy. "What the fuck is going on?"

Wordlessly, one of the men grabbed her by the hair. She sliced him away with a chop to the forearm, then pushed away another man who tried to grab her by the waist. She stumbled toward the hut door, only wearing her pajama pants and T-shirt.

Another man came at her. She punched him, then two came at her. One grabbed her around the waist while the other took her into a headlock. The man with his arm wrapped around her neck whispered into her ear. "Behave, then you will survive."

Naturally, Ryver did not believe this claim. She kicked the man's toes who had her by the waist while punching the man in the gut who had just spoken to her. He did not move and instead twisted her around by one arm and brought a knife to her throat. Her fear had returned, and she swore she could feel her heart slamming into her ribs.

"Do as I say," the man whispered. "If you behave, you will not die. Listen to me."

She was outnumbered. If she even tried to

fight, which she'd trained for so she wouldn't be scared in a war-torn country, they had weapons and would likely kill her before she could get any help. She complied, sliding her hands behind her back for them to cuff.

They forced her quietly into the back of a truck with a blindfold over her face. She wondered what had happened to the McKay's and tried not to panic. She sat in darkness for hours, bouncing up and down on the road, not saying a word, but planning, wondering, worrying.

Her mind had been frantically rattling when they finally stopped. The men roughly removed her from the truck, taking her into a small, enclosed area. Ryver could smell rust and shit. One of the men removed her blindfold, then threw her down to her knees.

It took her a second to adjust to the tiny lightbulb one of the men was holding in the corner. She looked around, trying to study her surroundings quickly. It was a shed or a shack of sorts, not particularly distinguishable. There were chains behind her and a pile of what was probably the source of the shit smell.

Christ, if her father could see her now. Why did she do this again? Oh, yeah, because she really wanted to help those in need. Her dad would encourage her to help somewhere in the U.S. but she knew the entire world needed help. Fuck, what a situation to be in.

As if reading her thoughts, one of the men took out a handheld video camera. Another forced her to sit up straight by pulling at her hair. The man who pointed to the camera bellowed instructions. "Tell your government you've been kidnapped, and we will only let you go if they send ten million dollars to this bank account." Another man held up a sheet of paper with a row of letters and numbers scribbled out.

She blinked heavily, trying to read the letters as she recited her pleas multiple times. Ryver could not believe the situation she was in. She did not cry in the video, despite the men's encouragement to be more emotional. She simply wasn't able to – she was too busy trying to survive. Somehow, she'd been able to close up emotionally. She didn't know how, but her survival instincts took control. *Stay alive. Stay alive.*

"That's good enough," the man holding the camera said as he closed the viewfinder and packed it away. "You stay here, and we will be back. Remember to behave."

"Wait," she hollered. "Where are the two doctors who were with me?"

The leader turned to her, face stoic. "Dead."

Her knees nearly buckled. This wasn't supposed to happen. This part of the African republic was supposed to be relatively safe. No rebel forces fighting for control of the government and no ruling drug lords.

She was yanked backward by her T-shirt, and old, rusty chains were wrapped over her wrists. Her captor locked them tightly, then retreated to the room with his other masked mates.

Instinctively, Ryver yanked at the chains. They were tight against the wall, and she clenched her fists and teeth to attempt to loosen them, even a bit. They didn't budge, and she fell onto the ground in defeat.

At that point, the urge to cry overtook her. There was nothing wrong with crying, but she found that it often clouded her practical way of thinking. She wanted to cry for the family she'd never get a chance to have. Helping others had been her number one priority and now she was going to die without ever being in love. God, she might never see her dad again. She'd never get a chance to hug him.

"I'm so sorry, Dad," Ryver whispered into the empty space. She heard a few clinks and clamors of mice scurrying around the room. She sighed – how was she going to get herself out of this?

She could either wait for the ransom to be paid – which rarely turned out well – or she could escape. The chains were tight, but they were old. Ryver was sure there was a way she could loosen them from the wall when she had the strength. *You've got this, Ryver. You can do it.* That's what her dad always told her when she was in school and stressed with everything going on. Or when her first boyfriend broke up with her because she was too busy with school.

But she was exhausted. She needed to rest before she attempted her escape because she also had no idea where they had taken her. She tried to track the turns of the truck as they had left the village, but it was too long a drive to know for sure.

She thought about how her father would worry when the government reached him. She would figure this out herself the way she always did. Her father had taught her not to depend on anyone. People had a tendency of letting others down. She didn't need anyone to help her out of the predicament she found herself in. She wished she could have the strength to get through this without crying.

Ryver closed her eyes, sitting on the floor of the shack. She heard nothing coming from outside, not even wildlife. Other than the rats that were moving about in the dark room, she was alone, and when she was alone, she could think and rest.

But before she knew it, she was falling away into the darkness of sleep. It was a comforting blanket after such a horrible day.

TWO

CANNON

Cannon awoke from his slumber to the sound of his dinner smacking the concrete floor in front of him. His eyes shot open to see a tray of slop spilling over the edges. He clenched his fists and growled at the guard walking away, chuckling to himself. "Oh good one, buddy, you think you're really original, eh, fuck-face?"

Cannon moved from his seated position against the wall and the chain wrapped around his ankle yanked. After two years in the Supermax, as the guards and inmates called this hellhole, he'd think he'd be used to it by now. Guess no one really got used to having their soul crushed every waking minute of the day.

The tray of food was just out of reach for him. He bellowed to himself as the tip of the nail caught the edge, then he was able to slowly inch it toward himself.

He picked up the tray, panting hard. That single movement had exhausted him, which was also a familiar sensation that he'd had to adjust to over the years of his confinement. He sighed with the tray on his legs. There was something moving in his meal, a bug of some sort, but that didn't matter. Cannon needed strength from wherever he could find it. He dug into his dinner and fantasized about the better days.

The better days of shifting were what Cannon longed for like a long-lost lover. He used to be able to shift at any moment he wanted, then fly toward the moon, leaving everything behind. There was great freedom there, and that was something he had lost within the past years. His dragon had been contained, shackled, in an invisible prison inside his head while he sat in a real one. Every now and then, he would touch the implant on the back of his neck lovingly as if to calm the dragon and to reassure him that his freedom was coming.

Except he didn't really know whether or not that freedom would ever come. He was a mercenary shifter caught fighting the U.S. government which made him "too dangerous to exist." The bug planted in the back of his neck stacked his nervous system back into a human pile, one that made him weak and often sickly. He had tried to remove it once – probably all of the shifters in the prison had tried at least once. But the consequences were beyond dire.

The echoes of pain from the removal of the implant still haunted him. It was like having your spine ripped out from the top of your neck to your lower back. He had been paralyzed for over a month while his spine and nervous system slowly healed. If he'd been human, he would've died on the spot. He feared that he had killed his dragon altogether. But he could still feel his faint whisper. He longed to release him and fly away, to thrive on some high mountain that touched the sky.

And be completely alone.

Cannon ate solemnly. Despite having lost the abilities of a shifter, he was still a mercenary and still able to detect danger. The danger was the sound of clicking boots approaching his cage. They weren't the sound of a casual night guard. No, these steps had meaning.

"Good evening, General," he said.

A woman with a thick frame approached his cage. She was small but clearly strong and experienced. She had aged since Cannon had last interacted with her but maintained an attractiveness very few could resist. He mostly did his best to avoid her because nothing good could come out of pissing off the prison warden.

He continued eating as he held her frame in his peripheral vision. With her hands behind her back, she spoke assertively. "Cannon, I have some good news for you."

"Do I finally get to die?" Cannon joked, but a part of him meant it. He'd rather not be living than sit here in a cage, unable to tap into the most authentic part of himself.

The general shook her head. "You're getting a chance at freedom, Cannon. I hope you can listen attentively to what I'm asking of you and what will be in store at the end of it for you."

Finishing his dinner, Cannon threw the tray across the side of his cage. He turned to her and raised his hands into the air, looking deep into her eyes. He shrugged, then let his hands rest in his lap.

The officer breathed in deeply, maintaining her soldier-stiff stance. "I am forming an elite team of shifters responsible for taking on some of the most dangerous missions known to man. Actually, they won't be known to men at all – it will be strictly shifter business and no humans allowed. Do you follow?"

Cannon nodded sarcastically. He was listening, but he never trusted anything this woman said. The idea of freedom did perk his interest, though, so he paid attention to any catch that was coming.

The general closed her eyes before she spoke. Cannon swore he saw the beginnings of a headache in her brain. "The first mission pertains to a group of doctors who have been taking care of children in Africa. They were kidnapped yesterday and are being held for ransom."

Cannon nodded seriously this time. "Why me? Why not send in the SEALS or whatever military groups you have?"

"We can't trust anything they're saying about a ransom. They're in the middle of an area full of extremely dangerous militia groups. One that no human would survive." She gave him a piercing gaze. "I know you've gotten out of worse situations than those."

Cannon tapped his fingers together. "Where does my freedom part come into play?"

"We will remove your implant." She raised an eyebrow. "Your dragon will be set free because it is essential to the mission. But you must successfully complete the mission, for true freedom, of course."

Cannon smiled wide. He hadn't smiled genuinely in years. "Of course."

"Once it is complete, you will be free to roam in shifter society. But because of your sentence, you would be bound to us forever. You understand."

Cannon sighed, then stood. He couldn't get himself all the way to the edge of the cage as the chain clanked in strain against the wall. He knew there was a catch coming, but it really didn't matter – he was high on the notion that he could let his dragon free again. Free to fly at a moment's notice.

He looked at her through the bars. It was difficult to see in the dark, and she was much smaller than him. But he knew she meant what she was saying. He wanted to make sure she knew that he meant what he was saying too.

"I will get your doctors. No problem at all."

The general sighed, then called one of the guards to release him from his cage and the chain. She turned to him as she waited. "This is a very important mission. One we cannot send even the toughest of our men into. So I am sending you." She met his gaze unblinking. "The one person who walked out of a major war between two countries and countless terrorist organizations at every turn, that would destroy the strongest of men. I hope I can trust you, Cannon. If you prove untrustworthy, then your dragon will never see the sun again. Do we have an understanding?"

Cannon gave her a single nod, and she turned and walked out of the cellblock, passing several guards on their way to his small prison. Cannon released an unintentional moan as the chain around his ankle was unlocked. He rubbed it.

The guards took Cannon to the same operating room where he had his bug first put into his neck. But this time, the experience was entirely painless. They used a device that looked like a giant magnet and placed it on the back of his neck. It powered up, then sucked the device off in a single swoop. Cannon almost instantly sensed his dragon come back to life. Blood coursed through his veins like fire.

Before he could move, another pressure poked at the same location, and something plunged into the opening. It stung a little, and Cannon cried out in surprise.

"Fuck, what the hell was that?"

General Anderson came over to the operating table. "We don't need you running off before you get the doctors. This is a suicide bug. It ensures that your head will explode if you go outside the radius of the mission. It also keeps you from fully shifting."

Cannon rubbed the back of his neck. "I thought you said you need me to have my shifter abilities."

"You have everything – strength, speed, hearing, claws, teeth. But no wings. You're not completely free yet, Mr. Dez." Nydia smiled, but there was pain behind it. Her hand lingered on Cannon's arm before she left the room quickly.

Sure, he'd rescue the doctors, but as soon as they were safe, fuck everyone else. He was out of here. The damn human race could all go to hell as far as he was concerned.

THREE

RYVER

Someone shook Ryver awake the next morning. She was baffled to find she had slept through the entire night and wasn't able to plan her escape. Ryver shook her head and found a woman waking her, one without a mask. She grabbed at her shoulders and sat her up from her slumped position.

"Here, these are for you."

The woman was carrying a bucket and toilet paper. With a look of sadness on her face, she placed it next to Ryver. She seemed to be doing as she was told but with little approval. She also had a water bottle in her hand and signaled to Ryver to raise her chin. Ryver did so and welcomed the delicious taste of water after a long night of horror. She chugged at it while the older lady guided the bottle into her mouth like a little lamb.

Ryver nodded for her to stop. She swallowed the liquid then inquired to the woman. "What's going on? Can you help me?"

The woman grimaced, then went toward a tray she had placed at the front of the shack. It had a bowl of oatmeal on it and some nuts. She placed it in front of her, then stood for a few solemn moments. She had her hands clasped together with concern. Ryver watched her, counting on her doubt. She pulled at the chains and whispered. "Please."

The woman's face completely lost color. Her eyes widened, possibly suddenly struck with the terror of what would happen to her if she didn't follow orders. She fled the room before Ryver could say anything more.

"Fuck." Ryver glared at the oatmeal. It didn't look the most appetizing and probably wasn't cooked with the utmost care. But her stomach was pressing against her ribs – she was starving. She decided to follow her logic of gaining strength, then leaned forward and scarfed down the meal. It wasn't as terrible as she anticipated, but perhaps that was because it was essential to her survival.

She was licking up the last of her meal when two men in masks entered the shack. They aggressively ripped the door open, and blasts of uncomfortable light stung her eyes. She squinted, still focusing on the last of her meal. She didn't know when she was going to get another.

"Stand up." One of the men ordered while the other pulled her to her feet. She swayed and quivered as she stood. The other man came at her with a knife, so she screamed as loud as she could.

The man behind her shook her by the T-shirt. "Quiet. No one is hurting you."

It took Ryver a second to realize what was going on. The man who was holding the knife grabbed a fist full of her long ponytail, then began slicing it off of her head. Ryver's hair was naturally curly, so it was easy to remove a large chunk. Her heart began racing as she watched an important part of her being angrily taken from her. She tried to hold back tears as he finished, holding the blond hair between his fingers.

The man holding the hair snickered underneath his mask. His eyes were a deep stream of hazel filled with violence and frustration. The man behind her threw her down by her shirt. The man holding her hair continued to stare at her. As he did, he brought the hair to his nostrils and breathed in deeply. Ryver's stomach stir with fear and disgust.

"You probably taste just as good."

The other man grabbed his comrade by the neck. As they turned to leave, the man with the hair gave it another sniff and pleasurably watched her grimace. The door closed behind them with a slam, and Ryver released a cry that came from deep in the wells of her heart.

"Jesus fucking Christ!" She shook herself, and the chains rattled against the wall. She was sure that some of her fingers had gone numb from sitting elevated in the same position for eight hours. She had eaten but perhaps had eaten too rapidly. The food was swishing inside her like a storm about to erupt.

She didn't want to vomit, and she needed that sustenance. Instead, she sucked back tears and bit down on her lip hard but it did nothing to stop the sob that ripped from her throat. She inhaled deeply and plopped herself down on the ground. Desperation grew in her chest. She stunk. She'd urinated while she they'd grabbed her by the shirt and desperately needed to bathe.

Ryver assumed the hair was going to be delivered to the U.S. government as a threat. But Ryver didn't want to wait for whatever else was to come. She didn't want these men to find any weak points in her. It took everything she had not to react to the creep smelling her hair. Who knew what else he had in mind?

Ryver wasn't going to find out. She needed to leave tonight.

Once she had gathered herself, she made a plan. She would slowly loosen the chains on the wall throughout the day. She wouldn't completely remove them because she wasn't sure when or if the men would enter and find her trying to get out. If she was lucky, she could get out in the middle of the night when no one seemed to disturb her.

If worse came to worst, she could always throw the bucket of feces at them if one walked in on her loosening the chains.

So that was what she did. She pulled at the chains lightly throughout the day, noticing them inching closer and closer to coming out of the wall. She didn't pull too hard, as she didn't want to yank it out completely until nightfall. The men only entered the room to throw her more slop and a water bottle one more time. The water bottle was open and spilled mostly onto the floor. But she managed to grasp at it with her feet, taking small sips to savor it.

When the light had faded from beneath the door, Ryver knew it was time. She did her best work alone and this was the ultimate time to show her own strength. She pulled at her left wrist and completely whipped the chain out of the wall. It clanked loudly on the floor.

"Fuck." Ryver stopped moving, sitting still on the floor for a few moments. A few men outside the shack spoke and laughed at something. But they did not approach. Thank goodness. When she didn't hear anything for several minutes, she worked on her right arm.

She clenched her teeth and pulled with all her might then heard something outside. She stopped, sat down, and stayed still. Someone was trying the lock but didn't seem to have the key. Her mind began running sprints as she considered the man who had smelled her hair. Had he returned to find her breaking out? Or worse. Her stomach recoiled at the thought of his words.

The metal clicked and clanked together, and before she was able to grab at the bucket, the door swung open.

FOUR

CANNON

Cannon took a military jet out of the States with another shifter who was being considered for the elite team. They all had their suicide bugs implanted. He may have been a shifter imprisoned for going against the government, but he was also a man of his word.

The team had to make their way through the country as discreetly as possible since multiple militia groups dominated every village and kept their eyes out for foreigners. They took jeeps along back roads and oftentimes had to avoid the many civilian cries for aid. There was a disease running through many of the villages, but the multiple militia groups did not allow their own citizens to receive proper care. Cannon had to hold on tightly to the back of the jeep, forcing himself not to shift into his dragon form and attack all of the terrorist organizations and save every innocent person who needed it.

It was the most difficult for Cannon when he saw women and children. He had no problem protecting them when the hand of a corrupt man came down on them. They were the usual victims in these situations. It was almost always men who spread violence and left the children and women in the wake of their destruction. It was predictable and frustrating.

But he had to focus on why he was there. Then perhaps, he could become his own vigilante-type shifter and help these people.For hating mankind, he sure was a damn softy. Shit, he hated that he cared.

After visiting the village where the doctors were last seen, it took them a day of beckoning heat to locate the camp that was holding Ryver. While at the village, he received the news that only the female had actually been taken. The males had been killed while fighting their captors.

Outside the kidnapper's compound, Cannon buried his backpack to retrieve after he'd fetched the female. He didn't need anything slowing him down. He wanted to get this over with. Cannon took it upon himself to be the sole infiltrator – he hadn't been directly asked. He carried a gun with him but knew that since his dragon's strength had returned, he wasn't going to need it.

"Just in case," his comrade named Gus had said from their jungle base location as he'd handed him the handgun. Cannon wasn't sure what kind of shifter the male was, but he was short with his features all scrunched together. Possibly a wolf or even a rat.

Cannon had laughed to himself.

"What's funny?" Gus asked.

Cannon shook his head as he stuffed food and extra clothing into his pack. "Nothing. Let's get this done and over with. I'll meet you at the trail north of the forest as planned. Got that?"

Gus grunted. Cannon pocketed his gun and adjusted his mercenary wear. Again, it wasn't entirely necessary, and if he needed to shift, he would only destroy the body armor. But he did as he was told without a peep of complaint.

Cannon secretly hoped he'd be able to shift. Even if it was just partial. And what the hell did "partial" mean besides no wings? He had been cooped up for years, unable to form into his true self. It was like wearing an ill-fitted suit, then finally finding that perfectly tailored one waiting for you. He craved that satisfaction.

Cannon checked his earpiece and left the jeep. They were set up miles away from where the female was held, so he made his way through the forest on light feet. His adrenaline pumped through him, and he loved the feeling. He hadn't been challenged in a long time, and a challenge was something that kept him feeling alive.

Cannon arrived at the wall of the kidnapper's camp, then swiftly hopped over it. The two guards on watch smoked cigarettes and laughed. They didn't notice him as he silently passed by.

He scanned the area, tapping into his night vision abilities he thought he had lost once the bug had been implanted in his spine. There were three tents set up and one rusted metallic shed. It was likely that Ryver would not be in a tent. Cannon scurried through the night air and found two men in his pathway.

He crept behind one of them, then silently snapped his neck in one quick motion. The other man barely had time to realize that his friend was dead when Cannon crushed his windpipe with his fist. Cannon moved the bodies into the shadows so they would only be found in daylight.

The shack was not far off. He noticed two more men sitting near it. One was dozing off in a lawn chair while the other played solitaire, flipping cards on the ground. Cannon groaned to himself. This wasn't even close to a challenge for him.

Cannon made his way around to the card player, then snapped his neck swiftly. The dozing man continued to snore. Cannon moved over to him, still crouching, then tapped his leg. The man's eyes shot open with fright, but he could not speak as Cannon choked the air out of his lungs. Cannon once again hid the bodies so others would not be alerted before they had the chance to leave.

He had made his way to the shack. There was a lock on it, one that he toiled with briefly, thinking perhaps if he picked it, he would be quieter. But after the sad excuse for guards he'd seen, he thought one loud metal slam wouldn't do him much harm. After attempting to pick the lock, he grumbled and tore it off in a single motion.

Cannon ripped the door open and saw a female in a battle stance, eyes squinting from the light of the moon. She was young, small, terrified, but ready to defend herself. A pang of sorrow filled him for her, but that rapidly morphed into respect. She looked so young and frail.

"Are you Ryver?" he asked in a hushed tone.

The woman stared at him without a word. She eyed him wearily and appeared to be in shock. The immediate sense of protection swept over him. He had to get her out of there and make sure she got home safe. Now.

"Come on. Let's go." Cannon outstretched his hand then heard her whisper.

"Shackled."

He moved to her, took hold of the remaining chain against the wall, and tore it from its hinges. It smacked down onto the floor loudly, and she cringed.

"I'm Cannon." He met her gaze and held it to let her know he was serious. "I was sent to get you. I'll get you out of here. Come on." He took her by the hand. She was only wearing a T-shirt and pajama pants. She was likely terrified and embarrassed. Cannon did not acknowledge the overwhelming smell of urine and feces as he guided her out.

Her hands were cold, and she held on tightly.

Cannon looked out beyond the shack. He could only see a few more men wandering about, but it seemed like no one had noticed his presence just yet. He tapped his earpiece.

"Home base," Gus said.

"Got her. On the way out."

Cannon glanced over his shoulder at his target. He couldn't stop the growing protective instinct taking over him. She was staring off into the moonlight and breathing heavily. He squeezed her hand and motioned toward the right side of the shack.

"We're sneaking out of here. You good?"

She nodded, not making eye contact with him.

Cannon knew there was nothing he could do at that moment to ease her fear. He wanted to hug her. To tell her he'd make sure she would be okay. That was too strange of an emotion to feel for a person he didn't know. So instead, he guided her out of the shack and motioned for her to crouch with him. They crept along the side of the tent. He motioned for her to stop, when to move, when to be quiet. She hadn't chosen a career in the military, but she knew instinctively how to follow orders.

Just as they were approaching the edge of the camp, a loud piercing alarm went off. This brought Cannon to life instantly. "Shit, we have to run."

FIVE

RYVER

When Cannon took her by the hand, Ryver instantly knew his strength. It was an odd thought to have in the middle of a rescue, but a nice one, nonetheless. He stood tall over her small frame as they moved through the compound. She was dazed from thirst, hunger, and fear, but she knew she was safe being near him. She noticed his slicked-back, red hair as he watched for guards.

He was very attractive. She shook her head, not believing she was thinking these things when she was just ready to escape people who were potentially going to murder her.

The alarm sounded and pierced through her

fantasizing mind. She noticed he had taken out his gun, then informed her that they had to run, but he would protect her with cover fire. She nodded, then a multitude of lights shot on around them in a circular motion. Suddenly, they were completely exposed.

"Go, run now," the man whispered as he pulled her through the entrance of the camp. He blasted the two men who stood in his way, their limp bodies falling to the ground like dolls. Ryver had no shoes on, so she could feel every cool edge of the forest floor as they smacked against it. The man was pulling her as they ran, seemingly in a certain direction as shots rang over her head, then in front of her.

They stopped abruptly in the forest. He pulled her to the ground. "Fuck. There's someone ahead of us. Damn it. We scouted this area already. It was clear. Stay here for a second."

The man crept forward to the point where he was only a shadow in the moonlight. Ryver heard shots and that familiar sound of bodies hitting the ground. He returned and took her by the hand once more.

"Come on. We should be fine..."

A bullet blasted past them through the tree

trunks and grazed Ryver's forearm, sending an involuntary cry out into the jungle. She glanced at her arm seeing her injury wasn't bad, more irritating than anything. There was another person ahead of them.

"Fuck, fuck," Cannon continued to whisper as he grabbed her arm, holding it down with great strength. He looked around frantically then grabbed her hand. "You're going to be okay, but right now, we have to change course."

As she watched, he stuck his hand into a pile of brush and dirt and pulled out a backpack. At least he was prepared, she thought.

The pain in Ryver's arm burned, but even she knew it wasn't life threatening. She ran with him as hard and as fast as she could. The man seemed to be running at an inhuman speed, one that she could barely keep up with. He noticed this and swept her up in his arms. She would've complained but he didn't even slow down while carrying her. She was grateful because she was seconds from falling behind. Terror pumped through her heart, and nothing tired you out more than fear.

The man kept looking back, seeming to check if they were being followed. The sound of bullets faded into the distance as they avoided them under the thick blanket of trees.

Finally, they stopped, and he put her down. Cannon had his hands on his knees and breathed out deeply. "There are no roads out here, so don't worry about hearing trucks. They can't get to us that way."

The world quickly tilted, so she sat on the ground. The man came to her and placed his hand on her shoulder, rubbing it. "Here, come over here." The man lifted her by the forearms and moved her to a nearby stream. He took off his backpack and pulled out a straw, handing it to her as she knelt by the river. "Here, this is a filter, so you don't get sick."

She took it wordlessly from him and drank desperately.

"Eat this," he said, offering her a protein bar. She had never wanted a protein bar like her life depended on it. She inhaled it quickly, almost choking in the process. After that, he handed her a small squeeze bottle. It had the words electrolytes on it. She figured she was definitely in need of those. She drank the entire squeeze bottle which was no bigger than her finger. Then had more water and leaned back onto the ground. She closed her eyes to focus on her breathing.

"I was sent to get you home safe," he said. His voice was still so soothing despite the anxiety threatening to take her over.

She opened her eyes and tried smiling. "I'm Ryver. I guess you know that already."

Cannon stuck out his hand. They shook, his palm warm. His smile was broad and alluring.

The sudden sound of swiftly moving helicopter blades caught their attention. Cannon looked overhead and sniffed the air. Ryver frowned, watching him home in on something Ryver wasn't aware of.

"The trees are too thick here. They won't find us. Don't worry."

"I'm not worried," Ryver lied. She didn't want Cannon to think of her as a damsel in distress.

He smiled again, making her feel weak in the best way. "Well, to be honest, I was a little worried." Their eyes lingered on one another for a few more moments before Ryver turned away, lowering her forehead to her knees.

"How is your arm?" he asked.

Ryver had completely forgotten she had been shot. Well, sort of shot.

She looked. It was barely grazed, only slightly bleeding. She shrugged. "Nothing too serious. I need to wash it off."

She eyed the stream. "Do you think I can do a quick wash? I feel disgusting and I smell horrible."

He nodded. "I'll have to stay right here. You're okay with that?"

She bit her bottom lip. "Would you turn just for a quick moment while I undress and then again when I'm ready to come out?"

He seemed to think about but agreed. "I'll grab you something clean while you wash." He handed her a small capsule. "When you wet it, it turns into a wash cloth with soap in it."

She gasped. "Thank you so much."

Once she'd had the fastest wash of her life and had rubbed the rag all over her body, face and hair, she submerged in the stream and allowed all the disgustingness of the time in captivity to wash away. She dried herself with one of his t-shirts and then put on a T-shirt and shorts he'd brought in his bag for her. She didn't know if he had any other clothing for her, but was grateful for the one clean set.

"Thanks for the clothes and the wash cloth," she said.

"You're welcome. That's the only set I was given for you so we need to keep you clean if possible."

"Yeah. I understand."

"Here." Cannon tossed her a first aid kit. "We don't need flesh-eating bacteria making a home in your arm."

Ryver was exhausted, but he was right. She removed a few bandages from the kit and then squirted medicine on top of her cut. It burned, but she knew it was going to help.

They intermittently heard the sounds of choppers overhead as Cannon pulled something small from a pocket and put it in his ear. "Home base," he said, then paused a second. "Plan B." When she saw his scowl, she wondered what the other person was saying. "Get out of there, Gus. Rendezvous with the A.L.F.A agent. We'll see you in Uganda. Out."

Ryver jerked with surprise. Uganda? She almost threw up then and there from anxiety. They were hundreds of miles from the border. "We can't walk to Uganda. It'll take a week."

Cannon's brow rose. "I have food for several days, and there are numerous creeks and lakes along the way." He held his hand out to help her up. "Plus, your abductor's compound happens to be much farther east than the village you were in."

"So, how long will it take to get there?"

He shrugged. "Barring interference, a few days."

That was not what she wanted to hear. Traveling several days through the jungle didn't sound like a good time to her. She winced. "God, how many snakes live in the jungles?"

He chuckled. "Many."

"It's not that I'm a wussy, but even my dad hates snakes. And aren't anacondas prevalent here?"

"Yeah. Especially in streams."

She squealed and rushed away from the water. "And you let me get in there?"

He laughed harder. "I would've known if there were any nearby. I wouldn't let anything happen to you."

She cleared her throat. "Good to know."

Cannon started hiking, and she hurried to catch up. She guessed they were headed east. She looked up to see stars through the leaves but didn't know any of the constellations here. Back home, she knew them by sight.

"You like the stars?" He asked.

"My dad spent many a night in a tent with me in the backyard, flashlight in hand along with a book showing me all the star groupings." She smiled and then sighed. "That was back when everything was good. When the only worries in the world were what daddy was cooking for supper." She snorted a giggle. "Usually, the meal included mac and cheese," she grinned at him. "My favorite."

"I like mac and cheese too. The cheesier the better."

She grinned. "Same." Then her smile fell from her lips. She missed her dad. When this was all over, she'd go home for a long visit. Her inner desire to help others had been satisfied for the time being. Now it was time to take care of herself and those she loved.

Ryver glanced up at the man in front of her. She marveled at how gracefully his body moved through the trees and over fallen logs. It was as if he floated while she made enough noise to rival a herd of elephants.

Now that her adrenaline drained, the pains in her body registered. Her shoulders ached from being chained, her wrists from the rough cuffs. And now... "Ow, shit." She hopped on one foot, trying to pull out whatever was stuck in the other sole.

Cannon stopped and looked back at her. "Damn. You don't have any shoes."

She shrugged. "Boy, aren't you observant?"

He scowled. "I had to keep us alive, which was much more important. He pointed to a downed log. "Sit there and rest a moment."

She wasn't about to argue with that order. With a sigh, she plopped down. When she looked up, Cannon was nowhere in sight, though the darkness didn't allow her to see far. She heard a branch snap not far in the distance. Her heart leaped into her throat. Had the kidnappers caught up already?

"Cannon?" she whisper-shouted. He didn't reply. Feeling like a sitting duck, literally, she crouched and scooted toward a thick tree. In the same direction came the sounds of thrashing leaves and breaking limbs. What the hell was going on? Was Cannon fighting one of her abductors? "Cannon!"

"Hush, woman," he replied, appearing from the darkness like he stepped out of a dark room. "We aren't that far yet." In his hands, he held several small sticks broken from little branches and a fist full of vines. "I told you to sit. What are you doing up?"

She shook her head and sat, watching Cannon layout several sticks side by side. Then he stripped the leaves from a vine and weaved it over and under the sticks like making a wicker basket. When he'd bound a flat six-inch rectangle, he wrapped the middle of a piece of vine toward the top and tied the two strands to the side of the rectangle. What was he doing?

He held the flat weave next to her foot. "Slide your toes here."

Then she saw it. "Oh my god, you made me a pair of wooden flip-flops?" She glided her toes under the strap. "That's so thoughtful of you."

He scowled up at her. "Yeah, don't tell anyone. I have a reputation to uphold."

She couldn't help the way the side of her mouth quirked up. He was a tough guy with a melted chocolate center. And now, for the first time in forever, her hormones decided to wake up and take notice. Like, really notice. She shook her head, wondering what the hell was wrong with her. She was drooling over some highly skilled military guy whose goal was to get her out and say good-bye. Not to mention, with his looks, he had to have a dozen women knocking his door down.

"Come on," he said, standing. "We have a long way to go before we can stop."

BY THE TIME Cannon finally called a halt to the march through hell, Ryver was numb emotionally and mentally. The sun hadn't made an appearance yet, but the area had begun to lighten.

Cannon raised his nose and sniffed the air. "We'll camp here for the day. Get some rest and start out again when it's dark." She couldn't do anything but agree with him.

She watched him as he removed the tent from his pack and built it between two small trees. It was also surrounded by bushes, so they would be less likely to get caught. He tossed branches and excess bushes on top of it. She wondered exactly who this man was and why he was chosen to save her.

Ryver wondered what kind of training this guy had because he did not slow down or even falter at any point. And when he carried her, he barely slowed down. It's like he was some super soldier or something. She shook her head. For all she knew this guy was just a very well trained mercenary.

At that moment, though, it didn't matter. Ryver had a splitting headache that she wanted to sleep away. The fact she could do it with this man seemed all the more comforting.

"All done," Cannon said as he stood with his hands on his hips, admiring his handiwork. "It's no Hilton, but it will do."

Ryver did not react to his jokes. She merely walked to the tent. She noticed it was small, probably meant for only one. But that didn't bother her one bit.

"You can get in first. I'll be okay out here for a bit."

Ryver turned toward him. "You should rest too. I'm hopeful they won't be able to find us."

She honestly just wanted him close to her body. He stood silently for a moment, perhaps picking up the subtext, perhaps not. "All right. If you are comfortable with that, of course."

Ryver climbed into the tent, curling herself into a ball. Cannon came in after, zipping the tent shut. He lay down behind her to the point where they were nearly spooning. Ryver had the urge to rub against his pelvis, but she managed to avoid it.

That would have been something she would do to entice a lover in entirely different circumstances.

She could smell him from being in the tent so close. He was sweating, but it wasn't a tangy sweat, but a strong, masculine one. The thoughts of him making love to her right then and there eased her headache a little. What in the hell? Why was she so thirsty for this guy?

An idea sprung. It had to be the fact she'd come so close to death that she was suddenly wanting a human connection, right? She hoped that was it, because she couldn't catch feeling for a mercenary who was going to drop her off at the safe zone and keep it moving. Her heart hurt at the thought. She needed to stop getting attached to this guy.

"Sorry about this." Cannon had placed his arm over her head so he had more room. He was obscenely tall, so tall that she was surprised his feet weren't sticking out of the tent. She smiled at the thought.

"It's fine. I just hope you're comfortable too. And, Cannon..."

They fell silent. Ryver could feel his stomach moving against her back.

"Yes?" he asked softly.

His voice almost made her quiver. "Thank you for tonight. I know the government sent you, and I know how difficult they can be to deal with, so thank you. I'm going to try to sleep now."

"Just doing my duty," he said quietly.

Ryver closed her eyes, leaning deeply into the warmth of Cannon's body. Just doing his job. If only his job consisted of more than just saving her.

SIX

CANNON

Cannon noticed that Ryver had fallen asleep almost instantly if her light snores indicated anything. He smiled and decided to close his own eyes. He didn't think he would get any sleep because he had to stay on guard. He had this need to hate her simply because she was a human. But the protective instinct and need to be near her was making him question himself. There was something different about her that he couldn't put his finger on.

Gus had informed him that Ryver had been in the country to take care of the children suffering from the disease that was running rampant. That was different from what many humans did...to try to make the world a better place. Perhaps she disagreed with old society ways. He thought this even before Ryver had thanked him for saving her.

Knowing she wasn't the typical human was adding to the emotional struggle he was experiencing about Ryver. He saw how strong she was trying to be and how grateful she was for him being there. He also sensed she wanted to be close to him. It was all making it impossible for him to hate her. He knew he couldn't. Something deep and strong woke inside him and let him know he had to care for her and protect her. That she was important to him.

He wished he could have shifted – things would have been a lot easier for him if he was able to simply fly out and over the trees with her. But no, he was to be kept on a leash.

It would be best to stay here for some time and keep an eye on her. He wasn't going to take a single chance of putting her life in danger. Relaxing, he took a deep breath and froze. Under the heavy smell of forest and odor wrapped around her, he picked out a familiar scent. It didn't even take a second for him to realize who it was very similar to – the one female he despised more than any other human...

General Nydia Anderson.

Fuck! His head spun with this information. How... what... did the general know who he was sent to rescue? She'd have to know.

What the hell was he going to do about this? What could he do? Immediately his brain said he should not like this female beside him, but his heart and dragon balked telling his brain to get over itself and shut the hell up. Ryver wasn't the general and he had to stop trying to hate her because of that woman. Maybe the general didn't know what was going on. He almost laughed at that. No, that was impossible. Of course, she'd know. He smelled the familial connected. Ryver was her daughter. She had to know. Why didn't she say anything? He was curious since Ryver didn't mention her either.

With a sigh, he closed his eyes for what he thought was a little bit, then realized several hours had passed. When he was fully awake he smelled some rabbits nearby and decided to hunt them some food. Sure, he could give her protein bars, but he'd rather give her some real protein if possible.

It took no more than a few minutes to catch and kill the rabbits. He returned to the tent, skinned and quickly made a small fire to cook the meat. He then decided it would be best if she were awake too. It would also be best for them to head out soon, just in case some of the militia that kidnapped her had made their way in their direction.

Cannon shook her lightly by the shoulder. She startled awake, sitting up and throwing an elbow into his chest. He couldn't help but laugh and feel impressed. This female could protect herself if need be.

"Don't worry," he said. "Everything is okay. I've been listening and there's been no sounds so far. It must mean they've gone in the opposite direction. But we should get going."

Ryver shook her head, thus shaking her out of her state. "Sorry. I think I was dreaming with meat. I could almost smell it."

Cannon smiled then proceeded to help her climb out of the tent.

"You weren't dreaming. I wanted to give you something solid to eat, so I went hunting nearby."

She blinked and followed him to sit by the small fire he was already putting out. He then handed her a large leaf with meat on it. "Are you for real? You hunted...for me?"

He grinned at her shocked expression. "Yes. It's just rabbit. I wanted you to eat something better than the protein bars I have. If I can't hunt much else the rest of the trip, at least you've had some good meat in you."

She blushed beautifully and made his heart thud in his chest when she gave him a dazzling smile. "Thank you. That's really kind of you."

They ate quickly and sighed after. He offered her a protein bar.

"Need one?"

She shook her head. "Probably at some point, but not now. That rabbit was amazing and I'm good for now. Besides, you're right, we should get going."

Cannon helped her out of the tent behind him. He figured she had to go to the bathroom, so he looked around the woods a few feet out so she could have some privacy. He motioned her forward, and she followed. He pointed out into the distance.

"You can do your business there if you have to go. No one is close to us, and I'll keep watch."

Cannon turned his back to her, so she knew he wasn't some weirdo who was going to watch her relieve herself. She went quickly, then walked by him to let him know she had finished. Cannon began packing the tent together when she asked for the filter straw. He handed it to her, and she thanked him.

She drank from the nearby river then offered it to him. "Why are you looking at me like that?" she asked. He lifted his brows.

Sticking the straw in the water, he said, "How am I looking at you?" He sucked up several gulps to stall as long as he could. He had so many questions he wanted to ask about her mother. When he turned back, she was holding his backpack.

She said, "I figured we can take turns carrying this stuff."

Was she serious? She was tired and had been held prisoner and still willing to take the load? This human was certainly not what he expected. And certainly couldn't be the offspring of the general. She seemed too kindhearted and personable.

He nodded to her suggestion, putting the filter into his pocket. He pointed to the woods. "We head east. We'll just take the trails until we can find some cover. Is that all good?"

She smiled at him, then began walking. "Sounds all good."

They walked through the night in silence. Cannon thought about making conversation but knew she was probably tired. But for once in his life, he was feeling talkative. He wanted to know everything there was to know about Ryver Fernando. Starting with how the general was her mother and why neither mentioned the other.

They kept going until the sun was about to rise. They came to a tiny village of a few people, and Cannon recognized enough of their language to communicate.

He asked them if there was anywhere he and his friend get some food and clothing, especially durable shoes. The people were friendly and kind, offering them an empty hut with a washroom. Cannon thought it would do for the day.

As they approached the hut, Ryver spoke up. "I'm sorry about all this."

Cannon shook, forgetting what she sounded like briefly. "You already apologized for that."

He opened the one door and guided her in. It was empty, except for a bale of hay. He opened another door which led to the attached washroom. There was a single faucet dripping water into a bucket.

"Can I take a quick shower?"

"Yeah I got a small bar of soap from the villager that sold me the clothes and shoes."

She grabbed the clothes, another bullet rag from him along with a new item he pulled from his bag. A small toothbrush the size of her finger. "Where's the paste?"

"It's already in it. Like the wash cloth. Just wet and brush and the paste appears."

She couldn't believe he had been given so many convenient items but was glad for it. He also handed her a small towel that would probably not dry her much but he'd been kind enough to buy those items for her along with some deodorant. She could hug the man.

After her ice cold wash, she was able to wash her hair with the soap and detangle it with a comb he'd gotten her. Having clean clothes and feeling clean did amazing things for her state of mind. It made her feel good. Hopeful. It also made her think of Cannon's body again. He was so big and strong. His smile made her heart flip and her hormones went up in flames when he was near her.

Cannon had closed the doors to the room and was sitting by the straw. "I'm gonna take a quick wash too." He went into the washroom and not five minutes later he was out in clean clothes, his hair wet and looking good enough to eat. Her emotional system went on full meltdown.

She swallowed hard. "I can't thank you enough. And I can't tell you how sorry I am."

He shook his head. "You've said that already."

"I mean it, though. I never would've survived out here on my own. I'm sure the military... or whoever... forced you into this."

"The military isn't really my business anymore." Cannon took apart the hay bale to create a makeshift bed, then he sat on it. He patted the seat next to him, and she came over. He noticed her scent waft close to him as she settled. She smelled good. Clean and the scent of Ryver herself came through loud and clear. He wanted her. Bad.

She sat with her knees up to her face. She was breathing lightly, which was a good sign. She looked at him, an expression of concern coming over her. Her eyes were the perfect shade of crystal blue. He lost himself in them, so he turned away.

"What do you mean?" Ryver asked.

"About what?" Cannon replied.

"You said the military wasn't your business anymore? So what do you do?"

His brows raised. "Besides saving doctors who get themselves kidnapped despite their good intentions to help?"

She rolled her eyes. "Okay, so you're an old-fashioned knight in shiny camo."

He chuckled. "No. Just your everyday mercenary." He snapped his jaw shut. He hadn't meant to tell her that. What would she think of him now? Did he want to tell her about his past if she asked? Shit, why did he care what she thought about him? It wasn't like he cared, right?

She raised her brows and leaned in. "A merc, huh? Do you have any family? Aren't they worried about you? I always worried about my dad when he left home when I was a kid."

Cannon shook his head. "No, it's just me now. I had family biologically, of course, but I lost them ages ago. I'm used to living alone. A lot of dragon shifters are."

Cannon realized he had just confessed to her of his shifter status. He whipped his head toward her out of fear, but her look never wavered.

Her eyes were wide with awe. "It must be something to be able to shift. It's always interested me."

"Have you ever met a shifter?"

Ryver shook her head. "I've heard about them, like everyone else, but never really interacted. You seem fine so far." She grinned widely. She looked just as beautiful as ever, and Cannon realized he was liking her more than he needed. Emotions he didn't want to acknowledge were growing with every smile she gave him. And then there was the tiny whisper he kept ignoring coming from his dragon. A whisper growing louder by the second.

She smelled like waterlilies and cinnamon.

Without another word, she reached out a hand to touch his face. Electricity zapped through his body, an extreme shudder that almost made his muscles seize. The whisper grew into a roar. *Mine.* A scary but hopeful thought crossed his mind – was she his mate? How had he had noticed that? All the years of having his dragon silenced must have made it take longer for him to connect with Cannon enough to let him know this was their mate. Fuck. Holy shit. Ryver was his mate. The general's daughter was his mate. His. Mate. And with every second that went by, the need to protect and keep her made his bond with his dragon stronger. He inhaled and her scent filled his lungs and desire pounded in his blood. *Mine.* This made deserting mankind a bit more difficult.

His heart pounded in his chest, and she ran a finger over the scar on his forehead. "It must be hard to be alone a lot of the time."

Cannon nodded, mesmerized by her voice and touch. He found himself leaning forward to get closer to her.

"I've been alone too," she whispered. "I find it easier to be alone. You can't be hurt or hurt anyone else that way." She was leaning close to him, and they both moved like magnets toward one another. The kiss was soft and light, like wind over water.

How could this be? How was he supposed to deal with this? Cannon's dragon shook to be realized, to take her on, to make her his. But his conscious-self shoved it down – there was a mission to be accomplished. Not yet. Fuck. It should be not ever, but now everything changed. Ryver. His Ryver.

Cannon pulled away before the kiss could grow more intense. Ryver looked confused and stared at him with her brows furrowed.

"We should get some food and then some rest. We don't know where the militias are at this point." He shot up from his seated position and walked toward the door.

"Yeah, you're probably right," Cannon heard Ryver say, her voice full of disappointment, as he left to retrieve their food. He cursed himself and their predicament.

SEVEN

CANNON

Though it seemed to Cannon that time had stopped when their lips connected, he knew, with alarming clarity, that they could not stay put. It was far too dangerous. They had to keep moving. He had to keep her safe.

After quickly breaking camp, and being careful to obliterate any traces they had ever been there, they set off walking at a brisk pace. He sensed that Ryver would have preferred to walk slower, but that would only be giving themselves up on a platter. He wanted to pick her up and carry her again, but she had already rejected the idea when he'd asked her not more than a few minutes ago.

Cannon was on his own with a woman who

drove him to emotion. That was fine with him – as long as he could keep his head straight.

Sure enough, his instincts about a hasty departure proved correct. The night was already well advanced, and his night vision was on high alert. Ryver walked in concentrated silence behind. Looking back, Cannon shot her a reassuring grin. The trouble was, he wasn't sure she could see it.

And that's when they attacked. One split second of letting his guard down was the exact moment that a flurry of bullets blazed inches from them, tearing into the nearest tree. White, pulpy tree innards billowed out in a grotesque parody of his own body were he to have been only a touch farther along the path.

Cannon didn't even blink. In one swift motion, he grabbed Ryver by the shoulders and thrust her to the ground, letting the thick underbrush aid in concealing her from further gunfire.

The bullets continued but only tore apart the surrounding trees and plants due to Cannon's quick movements. Any animals hiding in the leaves had long since vanished, leaving only the sound of searing metal.

Cannon did not waste his chance. With just a

thought, he unleashed the stopper that had held his dragon-self in check. All those years, those last few hours when freedom was just within reach, came to the fore.

He let it all go, and his dragon form burst forth. It was almost ecstatic, the purest, most vivid expression of self. A self that had been contained for so long.

His head elongated and morphed into a jagged taper of an angular dragon skull. Blood-red scales erupted over his skin that was rapidly widening and enlarging into four colossal legs, tipped by lethal talons.

The only things lacking were his wings. The general had made sure he wouldn't be able to fly away from the mission.

His transformation temporarily halted the bullets. Clearly, no one had anticipated such a reaction to a nighttime raid.

Cannon used the short reprieve to his advantage. Standing twenty feet tall, he used his height to better survey their attackers. There were six in all, and he surmised they were heavily armed and unafraid of a skirmish.

One attacker was positioned just to his left, in

the deep notch of a thick tree. He was easy to dispatch. The tree juddered and spat out its contents with a flick of his massive tail. From there, it was easy for Cannon to simply step sideways, feeling the body flatten beneath his powerful foot.

However, in moving, he discovered another attacker lying in wait who leveled a knife at his leg. Though it barely penetrated the thick scales, Cannon registered the prick of pain it extracted.

Twisting his head, he was able to knock the attacker to his feet, consigning the knife to a rusty end by being lost in the underbrush. After that, all Cannon had to do was slash at the exposed belly of the man with a talon. Shrieking, the man went from matte black to glossy black as his lifeblood spewed.

"That's no scratch," Cannon muttered to himself, turning to face three more attackers who were fanned out beyond his other flank.

These attackers were not about to take chances with trees or knives. They fully relied on the power of the gun. Bullets, a torrent of them, rained at Cannon. They must have lacked night vision, though, because many sprayed wide.

Small zings of pain erupted on Cannon's side and back as he crashed forward in pursuit. In response, the bullets continued, but he could see his quarry retreat. It was simply a game of cat and mouse now. Either they would fill him with lead, or he would crush them with strength. He was determined not to lose.

The closest attacker, a rotund-shaped man clad all in black, stood resolutely only fifteen feet away, the flare of his gun lighting up his face with every shot. But even he, with his pugnacious expression, retreated as Cannon came near.

And then, the attacker tripped – a fallen log in the exact right spot. Cannon was instantly grateful for the wonders of nature as the man comically fell ass over teakettle into the brush.

One quick snap of Cannon's jaws dispatched the man's bowling ball of a head from his body.

That left only two. They were close to each other, separated by only a few feet. As he approached, Cannon sensed their desperation rise. Bullets still flew up to greet him, but he used the cover of the trees to shield himself from most of them.

It would only take one small window, Cannon knew, before he could wipe them out. He just had to ride it out.

Sure enough, the moment came. One attacker

on the right suddenly stopped firing. By the insistent metallic sound that now issued forth, Cannon reasoned the gun had suddenly jammed. Cannon seized the moment, grabbing the man with one front paw. The guerrilla screamed in surprise. Cannon held him aloft for several terrifying seconds before whipping him around like a string.

The man's dizzying misery was ended when Cannon slammed him against his fellow attacker. Both bodies crumpled like paper.

A sense of immense satisfaction surged through Cannon as he surveyed the flattened and bloodied ground glinting brightly in the moonlight.

It was short-lived, though. A small cry made him turn. Shock quickly overtook Cannon as he realized he had missed one of the attackers. And he had found Ryver.

Turning on a dime, Cannon lurched toward her. He could see she was not defeated just yet. She had managed to find a sturdy log, and though the man scrambled to disarm her, she kept him at bay with several well-timed swings. He managed to dodge each. Cannon was still too far away to help. A howl escaped him in a fury.

The cry caused her attacker to turn to the sound. Just then, Ryver swung the log one more time, this time landing it squarely on her attacker's head. With a satisfying thud, his body fell at her feet.

She stood, for many moments, just staring at his inert form.

"Are you all right?" Cannon asked, pulling up to a stop.

In response, Ryver surveyed her body. She seemed to be in a daze. It was then Cannon saw it – a bright gash in her side, a fluorescent slash of wetness.

"Your side," he growled.

She looked down and winced. "Oh yes. I guess there's that." Looking up at him, she laughed quietly.

"You're a real dragon," she said, awe tinging her voice.

"That I am. Or can be," he replied, turning back into his human form. It was diminishing, but he needed the great gift of humans – opposable thumbs.

Kneeling near her, he inspected the wound. "It's not too bad. I've seen worse," he said, pulling out the first-aid kit and bandaging the injury.

"That's comforting," she said, gritting her teeth as he pulled the bandage tightly.

"Stay here for a moment."

She did so, resting back on the soft earth. Cannon shifted back once more to his dragon self. Using his talons and mouth, he quickly assembled the six bodies of their attackers and dumped them unceremoniously in a thick bush.

"Don't want to make things easier for our pursuers, now, do we?"

Ryver nodded, watching with unabashed fascination at his dragon agility and grace.

The bodies disposed of, he shifted back, dressing in clothes from his pack. "Think you're okay to walk?"

She stared at him wryly. "I don't have much choice, do I?"

He wanted to be soft with her and offer to carry her, but he knew that would only weaken her when he needed her to stay strong. "No."

And then they were off. Their progression was slowed by Ryver's injury, but she didn't complain. Or asked to be carried, which filled him with pride.

Soon, however, it became clear they needed a break. Finding a small creek, they stopped to rest and wash.

"I've soaked my shirt through with blood. And my pants. Gross," she said, crinkling her nose. Cannon tried not to find the expression cute.

"Let me see what else I got in here," he said, rifling once more through the pack.

"That thing never ends," she laughed, wincing at the pain it caused.

"Here," he said, holding out a T-shirt and sweatpants.

After removing her new shoes he got her, she pulled on the clothing to discover she was swimming in them. But there really wasn't much choice since the dirty outfit was the only one they'd been able to get from the villagers. All the villagers were smaller in size. Plus, the clean material was warm and sturdy. Tying the drawstrings tightly and rolling up the pant legs, Ryver made it work.

"Nothing makes me feel more like a grown-up than this outfit," she said, smiling broadly.

A distinct pain washed over Cannon. And he knew it was not due to the superficial injuries dotting his body.

It was Ryver's smile. Her beauty. She caused his very heart to constrict. It was like his heart was actually beating due to her smile. Like he'd been living with a hollow emptiness in his chest until now.

As she fiddled with the clothes to make them fit her small curvy body better, Cannon forced himself to look away.

He was there to save her, and he reminded himself not to sleep with her. Mate or not.

EIGHT

RYVER

Despite her injury, exhaustion, and hunger, Ryver somehow found the energy to put one foot in front of the other. She was cut off from her sense of self. Her leaden limbs, the painful ache that had settled in her injured side, and the hollowness of her belly were far away.

It was all due to the man-dragon that led her through the brush and trees. Though the night was only at its beginning, and they had already faced down a terrifying band of terrorists, Ryver knew they had many steps to go before they could safely rest.

She would have despaired if not for Cannon's calm and strong presence ahead of her. His night vision was invaluable, and she knew his protection was stronger than ever.

But was it something else that also compelled her? She was certain it was. For it was that feeling alone that kept her moving. Her utter confusion over her emotions about this incredible being. Her attraction – she could no longer deny it – confused her, as did her feeling of inadequacy in his presence. She was merely a human to his shifting greatness. That didn't stop the desire for him. And even more than that. She was like a teenager with butterflies in her stomach when he touched her or held her. When he'd smiled? It filled her heart with joy. It was surreal. She'd never experienced anything like that. She was getting to know this man more and more and her feeling grew the more she knew of him. How? Why?

What's more, she didn't exactly have room for anyone in her life right now. Hadn't she committed herself to saving lives in Africa? She had knowingly closed the door on any attachments and entanglements with that personal vow. Her heart was screaming out 'fuck that' and she desperately wanted to agree with that sentiment.

No, the man leading her – the man whose clothes she now wore clumsily like a small child, could not be in her life in a meaningful way. She simply had no room for it. *Make room. Give him a chance. Give love a chance.*

Common sense squashed that thought. Not to mention that survival trumped all else. There was no guarantee she'd even see another day. And so, like she was on automatic pilot, she trudged dutifully behind her man-dragon escort. After a time, Cannon slowed. Ryver knew that if she stopped walking, she might not be able to start again.

"Let's check that wound of yours," he said after verifying the area around them was terrorist-free. "Sit," he gestured to a large, flat rock covered in soft moss. Ryver was only too glad to do so, letting the rock take her full weight. The moss was cool and soft against her body.

With the utmost care, Cannon came to Ryver's side and gingerly lifted her T-shirt. The bandage was holding but could use a change.

"Lie on your side," Cannon instructed, placing a wedge of clothing on the rock to cushion her head. She could barely stop herself from leaning into him and seeking his touch. Despite her misgivings about the whole situation, Ryver found herself accepting each kindness from him. She needed it. She barely had the energy to resist anyway. Why not let herself be treated well for once? By the first man she more than wanted in her life.

Rustling through the bag, Cannon pulled out another bandage from the first-aid kit. The night air whooshed gently over Ryver's exposed skin as he removed the old bandage. Cool water followed, and though her skin was goose-bumped, it refreshed her tired flesh.

Soon, the clean bandage was in place, giving Ryver a sense of being reassembled in a very comforting way and swaddled, even. It was strange to be cared for, attended to while the dangers of the world swirled around her. And that it was Cannon the one doing it was absolutely perfect.

A LIGHT TOUCH pulled the veil of sleep from her eyes. Though a low-grade soreness pervaded her body, another feeling took precedence: warmth.

The moss beneath her was still soft and now thoroughly warmed by her heat. And the heat of Cannon. With growing awareness, she realized she must have drifted off after Cannon changed her dressing. Not only that, but he had also lain near her as she slept. In so doing, she had somehow migrated over to him.

"How did I get here?" she asked, a mix of curiosity and embarrassment in her voice.

"Funny thing, that. When I saw you were out, I laid back over here," he said, gesturing to the far side of the rock. "But you scooched straight to me. It was the oddest thing."

"I did not!" she protested, albeit weakly.

"You did! Would I lie?"

She looked into his face and realized that Cannon could do many things but lying was not chief among them.

"No, you wouldn't. I don't know how I know that, but I do," she acquiesced, smiling in the darkness. The night was in full swing around them, the darkness thick as a blanket.

"Guess what else I learned?"

"You learned something from lying on this rock?" she asked playfully.

"I did." He paused for dramatic effect. "You snore."

She batted at him, which made her side hurt. "Ow! I do not!"

"You do! I was worried I'd have to wake you. Someone might overhear you and attack."

Ignoring her pain, she swatted at him again. "Even if I do snore, it's not loud."

His smile flashed brightly in the blackness. "You're right. I made up that last part. You actually snore...in a very cute way."

The pain in her side dissipated, replaced by another type of pain. The pain of dead hope. Knowing there couldn't be a relationship between them but wishing things could be different. "Oh. Uh. Thanks." A moment descended between them, palpable as the night that flowed around them.

Cannon who broke it. "We need to keep moving. It's not safe to be still for so long. Are you okay to move?"

"Yes. Fine. Thank you."

"I can carry you," he said with soft look on his face that almost made her cry.

"No, I'm okay." She wanted his touch. Craved it. But she wasn't going to turn into a mess now.

And with that, they started walking. Cannon once again assumed the front of the line, and Ryver somehow found the strength to move her heavy limbs. The brief respite had helped, but she was nowhere near her old self. Did she even know what her old self was anymore?

At one point she found herself tripping only to be picked up by Cannon and into the warm cocoon of his arms. She leaned her head on his chest and sighed.

"You're too stubborn for your own good," he said.

She knew that. She rubbed her cheek on his t-shirt and then her nose on his throat before stopping abruptly. What the fuck was she doing. "I-I'm sorry. I guess I'm more tired than I realized."

"It's okay," he said, his voice thick. He glanced down and their eyes met and she raised a hand and caressed his cheek.

"Thank you. For everything."

He cleared his throat. "Stop thanking me. I'm not doing anything special."

She leaned her head back on his shoulder and sighed. "You'd be surprised how special all this is. I've yet to meet a man other than my dad that isn't interested in a woman giving up her whole career for him."

"Sounds like you've met some jerks."

She shrugged. "Yeah. But it wasn't just me. Even my friends. Most of the men we've dated are these big professionals, doctors and lawyers and they expect a woman to stop everything to be their girlfriend."

"That doesn't sound right," he grunted, holding her tighter.

"It's not," she complained, happy that he was in agreement with her. "My last boyfriend was in med-school. He thought because he had gotten a residency at a major hospital in California I was going to leave my life for his." She snorted. "He was angry that I would choose to continue my medical career than to choose to be his wife and personal assistant."

He chuckled and glanced down at her. "Let me guess. You were happy to disappoint."

"Damn straight."

"Yeah," he said. "I don't see you as being anyone's assistant. You're a leader. A survivor. A warrior."

She smiled at him and cuddled into his arms. "Thank you. That's the sweetest thing anyone has ever said to me."

He laughed and she felt it in the pit of her stomach. It warmed her to the bone. "So I guess that means there's no boyfriend waiting for you at home?"

She shook he head. "No." Then glanced at his

face. "What about you? No barrage of desperate females breaking down your door?"

He met her gaze and her hormones went on full alert. "No."

Oh, hell. He was single and so sweet and kind and fucking hell she wanted him. But this wasn't the time or the place, right? Right? After a few hours she asked to be put down. She'd gotten enough rest and could walk.

They walked the rest of the night. With each passing hour, the cloying blackness seemed to wane, becoming diluted with the approach of silvery dawn. The oncoming light was comforting, but Ryver knew she couldn't put her faith in it. They crested a small hill, and Cannon scanned around them before proceeding. "So," he said, "What brought you here?"

She let out a breath. "Thought I could make a difference. Help out in the villages. Bring some health to those who needed it."

Cannon nodded. "I like that. It certainly seems like they could use it. I'm sure your family will be glad to have you back."

A pang hit her heart. "It's really just my dad and me," she replied, her mind going to her parent and the guilt that filled her for making him worry so much about her.

"What about your mom?" he asked.

"I don't have a mom." The one photo she'd seen of her mother flashed in her head. It was of a younger version of her father with a beautiful blond, both dressed in camo, smiling widely. They looked so much in love. Her father kept the picture in a drawer. After so many moves and years, he no longer put it on his bedside table.

Cannon abruptly stopped and turned to her. "What?"

She lifted her hands. "Okay, technically, I had a mother since I exist, but she was killed shortly after I was born. My dad raised me as a single parent."

An expression of shock and disbelief crossed his gorgeous face. "What about aunts?"

"I have uncles on both sides, but I've never met anyone on my mother's side of the family. We moved a lot with dad being in the military. So we were never close to visit." She didn't mention that her father wouldn't talk about her mother's family. Thinking about her mother tore him up too much, so Ryver learned to live without knowing much.

"My dad was the one who taught me to never

show fear and to be strong in the face of adversity," she sighed. "Though I don't think he ever expected me to be in this situation. He did get me self-defense lessons as a kid, but that was part of the growing up stuff. I forgot most of it once I went to college and then med school." She gave him a serious smile. "I can still kick ass though."

He chuckled and nodded. "I'm sure."

The conversation ended abruptly when it was clear they had reached the end of the forest. Putting out a hand, Cannon gestured they were to walk very quietly and carefully. By now, the silvery light had surrendered entirely to the rays of buttery sun that fell lazily out from almost cartoonish clouds overhead.

Beyond the thickness of the trees lay a field of soft tall grass. And beyond that, the pitch of a brightly colored barn reached skyward. A small figure that appeared to be a farmer emerged from a side door. He stretched his arms wide in a movement that seemed, to Ryver, that he was welcoming the new day. She decided to take this as a good sign.

Upon seeing all this, Ryver instantly wished to be within the safety of the barn's walls. The thinning forest, the brightness of the day, it was too much. She was much too exposed.

"Let's approach with caution. If things go to hell, I'll handle it," Cannon whispered. With that, they left the relative safety of the forest and crossed the field. After finishing his stretches, the farmer easily spotted them and met them as the field tapered to shorter grass and dirt surrounding the barn.

The farmer spoke in a language she didn't know, his voice thick and gritty like he'd eaten some dust. He was not very old, but hard work and prolonged exposure to the elements had aged him like leather.

Cannon replied in the same language, pointing to the barn. He must be asking if they could stay there for the daylight hours.

The farmer mulled on it for a few moments before nodding. Ryver knew a surge of relief at that small gesture.

They entered the side door of the barn and were instantly enveloped by the smell of warm, fresh earth.

Choosing a pile of hay near the central wall of the barn, Ryver soon made herself comfortable and, before she knew it, had surrendered to sleep once more.

It did not last long. With a jolt, she woke. The sleepy barn was sleepy no more. The clack of loud footsteps, accompanied by the shouts of men, banished any shred of sleep.

Something was wrong. Dangerously so.

NINE

CANNON

Inside the farmer's barn, Cannon lay next to the extraordinary woman he'd rescued. His mind still spun with questions about the scent his dragon detected. She was definitely the general's daughter. The same one who had imprisoned him for the past years.

She was the warden's daughter. Could he still love her? The mating bond was one of the strongest forces on the planet. Would he be able to ignore it and live his life on his own terms? Well, he was glad the females weren't closely related. He should rest now.

No sooner had Cannon's head hit the bundle of hay he had assembled for a pillow, when he was snatched out of sleep by the sound of bangs and footfalls.

He knew instantly those were not the sounds of a regular workday on the farm. Shouts, the sound of heavy boots and distant heavy machinery told him they had been discovered. It didn't take long to discover just how.

"In there," the muffled but distinct voice of the farmer was heard, followed by, "you'll pay me now, right?"

They'd been betrayed. Cannon could guess that the sum was a pittance to the terrorists but a windfall for the farmer. It was a vicious cycle in places like these. Loyalty was cheap. So were the vows of men.

All vestiges of sleep left him as he sprang into action, desperately looking for somewhere he and Ryver could hide or use to escape. But, as he looked, dismay filled him. Nothing but dusty walls, towers of hay bales, and no windows to speak of. They were trapped.

Ryver, by this point, had also awoken and looked to him with a mix of fear and determination. Though the situation was dire, he couldn't help but admire her courage in the face of it all. She was hell-bent on not showing she was a victim.

They were lying on a stretch of bales about ten feet from the barn floor. He thought that might give them an advantage, but he was immediately met with a full display of guns as he peered over the side to get a closer look at the main and side doors. At least four thugs were standing there, a collective look of smug triumph etched into their bland faces.

He couldn't believe it. The farmer had not only sold them out, but he'd practically highlighted their exact location. If ever he got the chance, he would have to pay a special visit to the farmer to thank him for his hospitality.

Cannon knew he had to fight even in the face of being outnumbered and out-weaponed. Closing his eyes for a brief second so he could transform, he was struck back into reality when a metal pipe connected with the side of his head.

Stars danced and jigged around his sphere of vision, and he fought with all his might to retain consciousness. Yet, against all odds, he knew he had to stay awake. For at that very moment, Ryver's screams tore at his ears. If only he could stay awake. If only he had never fallen asleep in the first place.

It was a losing battle, and blackness overtook him.

HE WAS BACK IN PRISON, lying on the filthy floor, his teeth gritty with dust. Stiffness pervaded his every limb, and he wondered briefly how it was he still was able to breathe. His first thought was that he had failed so utterly. They'd had no choice but to exile him once again in this miserable place, never to see the light of day again.

He deserved it. He'd had one job, and he had botched it. There was no way he could be trusted with anything ever again.

"Water," he croaked, hoping one of the guards would hear him. Nothing happened. "Water," he said again, this time with as much volume as his dry throat would allow.

Still nothing.

That's when he noticed the ropes. The stiffness in his limbs wasn't due to the cold floor, although that certainly didn't help. It came from the ropes that bound him. He was hog-tied, his ankles raw with the rough twine. They rested almost behind his head, and his shoulders were stretched behind him in an agonizing position.

He was not back in prison at all. At least not the Supermax. He was in another prison entirely. And though he was no stranger to incarceration, his anxiety rose. The power of prison was always the unknown. Who were his captors? What could they do to a person? What were the rules?

At least at the Supermax, he had been there long enough to know the routine of the place. Which guards were friendlier than others. What meals to expect on which days. Lastly, which rules not to break.

This was another situation altogether. He had woken here under the watch of unknown captors, with a set of rules he had yet to learn. Such places could make a person die very quickly.

Cannon allowed himself a moment to close his eyes once more and gather his thoughts. He did not know where he was. Worse still, he did not know where Ryver was. Nor did he know how long he had been unconscious. A healthy goose egg had risen on his temple, and he suddenly recalled how he had received it.

He could only hope that, wherever Ryver

was, she was unharmed. Everything in his soul ached to think she could be in pain. Or worse.

"You tied the ropes good and tight, yeah?" a voice said. Cannon concentrated so he could hear with more precision. The voice had come from just outside his prison cell. His captors were close.

"Course, I did. You think this is my first time doing this?" another voice said. It was higher in register and seemed insulted by the insinuation.

"Settle down. I was just making sure. We are not even sure what we're doing with him yet. Rumor is he might be good ransom material. Who the fuck knows?" the first voice said.

"He's a big fucker. That I can tell you," yet a third voice said, followed by a grunt of what Cannon surmised was the fourth captor. "Took us ages to drag him in there."

So, they were confused about what to do with him, and they knew he was no ordinary prize. That's when the thought hit him. He was no ordinary prize, indeed. He was a shifter.

Closing his eyes once more, he willed the pain in his body to subside. Then, with a flick of his thoughts, he ordered his hands to change. Though sluggish, the transformation to large dragon claws began. As it did, the ropes binding him snapped like dry twigs.

He was certain the sound they made – of whips zinging through the air – would alert those congregated outside his door, but they were too caught up in their conversation to notice.

His bulk as a dragon took up almost every available inch of the small cell. Now free, he shifted back to human form – it was, for once, more advantageous in this situation.

The room was bare, made up of a stone floor and walls. Not even a cot or a bucket. Looking up, however, he saw one flaw in the design. A flaw that helped him immensely.

In the ceiling was a small hole. It may have been a place for a vent or electrical source at one time. Either way, it was the escape route he needed.

Ignoring the bands of pain that tore through him, he jumped as high as he could. It took several attempts, but eventually, his fingertips made contact with the raw lip of the hole. From there, he pulled himself up.

A shaft just large enough for his body snaked out before him. With utmost care, he crawled forward, making sure he made no noise, the sounds of his captors floating up to greet him.

He knew he was now directly overhead. A vent in the shaft proved him correct. Peering down through the slats, he could make out their forms – four in all, two were sitting, and two leaning against the wall. A grubby, beat-up wooden table and two chairs were the only pieces of furniture.

Cannon closed his eyes once more. His next move would be all about the timing. He took several deep breaths, counted to three, and punched downward.

The vent gave way like tissue paper, and he plunged forward through the hole it made. As gravity had its way with him, he shifted.

Hollers of surprise and anger rang out as his bulk overtook the room. The man sitting directly underneath the vent never had a chance. Cannon's heavy dragon chest crushed him instantly.

The others, however, had a moment to scatter, and they quickly established positions in three corners of the room.

Cannon stood on the remains of the shattered table, blood oozing from the victim at his feet. It was, he had to admit, quite the entrance.

A sharp pain, however, reminded him this was not yet over. One of the trios had struck him in his tail. In response, he flicked his tail upward, catching him on the chin and knocking him backward. If he survived, he would have one hell of a headache in the morning.

That left only two. One stood on Cannon's left and the other on his right. He had to wait to see who would show their hand first.

The one on his right pulled out a switchblade and raised it high above his head. He must have known how tough dragon skin could be to penetrate. Cannon turned the tables on him in that second, where both hands were raised.

The man plunged downward...into nothing. Cannon had shifted and stood naked as the day he was born.

Using the man's confusion to his advantage, Cannon kicked out, striking him in the solar plexus. With a great exhalation, the man shunted back and hit the wall behind him with full force. He crumpled to the ground.

That left only one.

Cannon turned to him and was met with a punch that made him see stars. This one was big, with meaty hands and red jowls. As Cannon reeled, the man got one more punch to his stomach.

Cannon groaned, backing up as the man approached. But he knew better than to stand right away. Letting the man think he had the advantage could help him.

The man approached, closing the gap between them. Cannon surged forward, his shoulder connecting with the man's soft belly. It knocked the wind out of him, and Cannon was able to push him across the room until they hit the opposite wall with a satisfying crunch.

The man, not one to give up easily, raised his fists once more, but Cannon was ready. Deflecting a right hook, he caught the man's jaw with his other hand. The man's head twisted at a painful angle, and he went down.

For several seconds, Cannon stood panting, reveling in his quick thinking. But he couldn't savor it for long. Ryver had still yet to be found. He eyed his backpack next to the door. Time to find his mate.

TEN

RYVER

Rough hands shoved her forward. She would have fallen flat on her face had her gruff escort not pulled her back in time. She wasn't grateful to him for the gesture, however. He was the one who shoved her in the first place.

Her hands were bound behind her back, and when he jerked her, intense pain tore through her shoulders. She dared not think about whether the injury in her side had re-opened. It was likely, but she told herself firmly to ignore it. Her whole body ached, so it was easy to disregard the specifics.

However, what could not be denied was the fact that once again, she was in a prison camp.

Not exactly bucket list accommodations, and now she'd been subjected to it two times in as many days.

Soon the ragged group reached a small building. From all appearances, nothing good ever happened within its walls, and Ryver tried to keep her eyes on the ground. They entered, and she was immediately shoved into a small cell that had little more than a floor and rickety bare cot. What with the blood all over and the urine and feces smells, it left a lot to be desired as a place to stay.

Her escort, flanked by two other thugs, pointed gruffly for her to position herself near the steel pipe that weaved up the corner of the cell.

"Back against it," he ordered.

She turned slowly and faced her captor. His rank breath streamed over her, and she held her breath while he reached around to connect the rough bonds that tied her wrists together to the pipe.

In so doing, he had to get awfully close. Ryver tried to keep her mind focused elsewhere as his pasty body rubbed against hers. She didn't want to give him any satisfaction of being repulsed or otherwise. She just wanted this whole transaction over as quickly as possible.

The ropes secured, he pulled his body back. In so doing, he let his hands drift over her breasts. It was deliberate. No geometry in the world, from her angle, would have meant his hands would be anywhere near them. But he meant to do whatever he wanted.

Something deep within her snapped. Before she could stop herself, she brought her knee sharply up. It connected with a satisfying thump into his crotch.

"Gah," he yelled, folding in half.

His cronies, standing near the cell entrance, doubled over in laughter.

The man finally righted himself and stared at Ryver. She looked past him like he wasn't there.

"You be sorry," he grumbled in broken English. Ryver pretended not to hear. It took all her effort not to spit in his face. That, she knew, would be a step too far.

Mercifully, they left after that exchange, the echoes of their laughter pinging off the bare prison walls.

It was only after the laughter subsided that Ryver allowed herself to take a full breath. Terror and revulsion coursed through her, and she broke into ragged sobs. It didn't last long, however. She refused to let it overtake her.

Instead, with one foot, she managed to pull the cot near to where she was positioned on the pipe and lowered herself down.

Awkward and uncomfortable, Ryver dropped her head to her chest, closed her eyes. Fear for Cannon filled her. She'd tried to warn him when a soldier swung a pipe at his head, but she hadn't been quick enough. She panicked when he fell unconscious. She didn't even know shifters could be knocked out.

Suddenly, screaming and the sound of metal ripping and wood splitting brought her back to glaring alertness.

Straining against her bonds, she tried to make sense of what she was hearing. Soon, a picture formed, and it lifted her spirits while it also caused her to feel a pang of worry.

A fight was going on – an intense one. Bodies crashed, and furniture was being torn apart. Only one person could take on several people at once. And that was Cannon. She heard a dragon fight, she was certain. Hope and anxiety sat side by side within her as the fight continued.

Meanwhile, she worked at her bonds. She had to find him, help him if she was able.

Furiously, her fingers pulled, rubbed, and pulled again at the rough hemp. The flesh on her fingers was soon shredded and bloody, but she didn't care. She had to free herself. The fight just beyond her cell told her nothing about who was hurt and who was dead.

With the last tug, the ropes finally gave way, and a rush of relief ran through her aching shoulders. Springing to her feet, she looked around for any sort of weapon. The cot, made of nothing more than pieces of metal, was designed to fold up, and the legs could be removed. Wrenching a leg off, she held its satisfying heft in her palm. It was perfect.

Approaching the door with caution, Ryver noticed with a shot of alarm that the sounds of the fight had gone silent. Was Cannon still alive? Was he hurt and bleeding on the floor just down the hall?

Her hand upon the door handle, she told herself to be ready for anything – including the sight of Cannon's dead body.

Just then, the door jerked open, and she was greeted by a bruised, bloody Cannon. Sweat glistened all over, and Ryver only barely averted her eyes in time.

"You're okay!" he said, his voice breathless with exertion.

"I am," she replied. What she didn't say was the rush of relief her heart filled with at seeing him alive again. Though her feelings were confused, not wanting to want him and there being a lot more than mere desire in her heart for him, she didn't think she could bear the sight of seeing him seriously hurt or worse.

"Good. We have to go. Now." His eyes traveled over her, taking in her condition. They caught on the metal bar still gripped in her hand. "Take that. We may need it."

"Sure...uh, yeah," she stammered.

With that, he turned, giving her another show of his gorgeous backside as he sauntered out of the cell. It was clear he didn't feel any sort of shame or awkwardness when it came to being naked in public.

A brief smile played over Ryver's lips as she thought to herself that if anyone had a body like that, they should have no problem flaunting it.

Her musings didn't last long. They were still very much in danger.

The small prison was empty, apart from the broken bodies they left behind. Harsh sunlight greeted them as they pushed the heavy metal door open.

"Aren't you going to put on clothes?" she asked.

"Don't have any more." He hefted his pack over his shoulder. Would she have to spend the next few days with this perfectly naked body leading her through the forest? God help her and her womanhood.

Cannon stepped outside. Peeking just over the tree line, about half a mile, Ryver spied the top of the barn where they had been discovered.

Cannon shot her a look. They didn't need to speak. They both knew what had to happen next.

Taking off at a rapid trot, they covered the distance within a few minutes. Just before the barn and accompanying house loomed into view, they slowed to survey the driveway. It was free of vehicles save for one – a rusty truck.

It was a good sign. Still, as they skirted the edge of the driveway so they wouldn't be spotted from the house, Cannon urged them to be careful.

Once they were at the door to the house, Cannon indicated that Ryver was to stand sentinel outside. He would go in first and check it out.

Nodding, she poised herself by the side of the door and held the metal bar in her hands, luxuriating in its weight.

Cannon silently disappeared inside. Ryver caught one glimpse of the dirty soles of his feet as he stepped carefully into the gloom within. She only hoped no harm would come to him.

A mere thirty seconds passed, which was an eternity to Ryver, before the farmer stormed out of the house backward. Ryver surmised he had been more than a little surprised to see his former guest reappear – completely naked – to pay his respects.

Ryver didn't let him wonder long. Before he even knew she was there, she brought the bar down on his head with a satisfying crack. He crumpled in a heap in the dirt.

A second later, Cannon poked his head out of the door.

"Come on in. Let's get stocked up."

The house was indeed empty of thugs and turncoat farmers. It was also furnished and fully supplied. It irked Ryver that this farmer seemed more prosperous than his neighbors. Why did he feel the need to sell them out then?

She didn't spend too long thinking about it. Satisfaction came in the form of filling a bag with food, warm clothes, and other essentials. He was paying them back for his shoddy treatment of them, whether he wanted to or not.

With some tearing and ripping, Cannon found clothes that managed to fit over his large frame. Finally, he came to something resembling a rest.

"Wish we could stay, but you know we can't." His tone was almost wistful.

"I know. At least we got a decent haul."

He looked at her, his eyes sparkling.

"That we did. Let's go."

And with that, they left the home with the farmer still crumpled in the dirt. They knew the new bad guys would soon return. They had to put as much distance between them as they could.

ELEVEN

CANNON

Cannon was tired but also riveted by the fact that he was now quickly able to shift into his dragon form. He loved coming into his own, fitting back into his own skin. He was invigorated.

But combined with that excitement was confusion about his feelings for Ryver. He knew that he was incredibly attracted to her, and clearly, she was to him too since she was the one who kissed him. Her ability to take care of herself and not require anything from him was also incredibly attractive. He watched her as they fled the guerrillas, keeping herself safe from harm and defending herself heroically.

"Are you okay?" Cannon asked. He knew

the answer he was going to get before he even inquired.

"Peachy." She kept looking behind her, ensuring there wasn't anyone coming after them. For a while, they focused on getting ahead.

Eventually, they stopped at a stream for a break and some water. As Cannon was taking his turn, he stopped and looked at Ryver, who saw him sitting at a nearby log. "I can shift into my dragon and carry you for a lot longer than in my arms if you're feeling tired."

Ryver gave Cannon an intense scowl. He figured he would get this reaction, but he wanted to reach out and ask anyway. "I'm fine, don't worry."

He shook his head as he drank from the river. He stood and put the filter back in his bag. "You know, that's called just caring about someone. I don't think you're weak in the slightest degree. I just thought maybe –"

"You don't have to think that. I'm fine, honestly."

Cannon wasn't the type of person who was going to be put off by her blunt reactions. In fact, it had quite the opposite reaction. It made him want her even more.

Instead of responding, he merely pointed in

the opposite direction that she sat. "I'm sensing there's some kind of cave near a stream in this direction. I think we should head over there."

Ryver stood without a word, smirked at him, then headed in that direction.

They walked, following the stream for most of the night, saying very little to one another. Cannon thought this was best. The sexual tension between them was way too intense, and he didn't want to encourage it even more at a time like this. She held her own and stepped quietly over branches and fallen tree trunks with ease.

As the sun crept over the mountains, Cannon saw the cave. It sat just below one of the majestic mountains with a tiny opening around the side. Very few would likely notice it. Cannon guided Ryver inside with his flashlight so she could see where they walked.

When they found a darkened flat area that was safe, Ryver pointed out toward the stream they'd passed. "I'm going to wash up first. Then I'll be back in a few. Ok?"

Cannon gave her a thumbs up, then felt like an idiot. His emotions were making him act like a fool. A part of him wanted to peek out of the cave and watch her. That would be a sight to see. But that would also be a way to get on her shit list if she caught him. Instead, he started a fire and waited for her return to go hunt them some food. Protein bars were okay but he'd seen more rabbits in that area than before.

When she returned, the fire was roaring. Her hair and face were damp, and she looked stunning. Her ocean-blue eyes glimmered in the firelight. Cannon tried not to stare too long and stood. "I'll be right back. I saw some rabbits by the stream. I want to go hunt quickly to get us some dinner."

Her body perked up. "Rabbits again? That sounds delicious."

He nodded and headed out of the cave. It was a fast hunt and he skinned them and got rid of the skin and blood so they wouldn't attract any other animals into the cave. When he got back, he put them on the fire to cook. "Watch these while I clean up. I won't be long. They should cook pretty fast and we can eat when I get back."

Ryver looked up and smiled at him. "Be careful. Also, it's a lot chillier than I thought it would be. Do you have a little towel?"

Cannon shook his head. "Don't worry. I'm a natural human furnace."

Ryver giggled. "Oh yes, I wouldn't dream of worrying about you."

As he left the cave, Cannon couldn't stop smiling to himself. By the stream, he removed his clothes and rinsed his body in the river. She was definitely right, and it was far colder than he had anticipated. He thought about her taking a look at his naked body just outside the cave where he couldn't see her. The thought filled him with warmth.

He returned to her in damp clothes but without his shirt on. He noticed her looking at him when she thought he couldn't see. He grinned to himself, filling with anticipation and a sensation of love he had yet to embrace.

Was this what it was? Love? He knew he wasn't here to have sex with her, and he was supposed to save her. But it was becoming increasingly difficult to avoid showing affection for her, especially since it seemed to be mutual. He wanted to hold her. To hug her. To kiss her. He wanted to let her know everything would be okay and that he'd die before he let anything happen to her. But more than anything, he wanted to tell her he wished they could spend more time together after they got back home. That they could be a couple.

He realized at that moment he didn't just want her physically. He wanted a relationship with Ryver.

"If only my father could see me now."

Cannon was stoking the fire when she perked up. "Why's that?"

Ryver sighed. "This is far closer to a military situation than a doctor would generally find themselves in, don't you think? My dad wanted me to go into the military so badly."

Cannon sat back against the wall of the cave, watching her ruminate. "Why do you think your father wanted you to be in the military? Wasn't being in it himself enough?" Or was it because of another reason?

Ryver crossed her legs and looked directly at him. Eye contact with Ryver was intense and beautiful. "It's a single-child syndrome. Parents want their children to follow in their footsteps to achieve the dreams they never could. He said I could do so much with my creative thinking." She rolled her eyes. "But it always seems far too conniving for me. Every country claims their military exists for some patriotic reason, but really, it's all about violence and manipulation."

Cannon nodded. She wasn't wrong, but being a mercenary was really all Cannon knew. A life of benevolence was so far outside his understanding.

As if hearing his thoughts, Ryver's eyes widened. Maybe it had escaped her mind for a moment that Cannon was a part of the military. "It's not that I think everyone who is a part of the military is like... bad. I know there are people with good intentions."

Cannon smiled. "I know what you meant. And you aren't wrong. It often attracts gun-toting lunatics more so than the Mother Theresa types."

Ryver nodded and crossed arms. "What about you? Why was the military a draw to you at first? Why not become a dentist or office worker?"

Cannon sighed. No one had ever deeply inquired about his military background. And if they did, he would usually lie or change the subject entirely. But he wanted to be open, for the first time in his entire life, with Ryver. "It was something I could do on my own. Any other career path seemed absurd to me, so I thought perhaps I could use my shifting abilities to help people who needed, I guess, 'extreme intervention.'"

Cannon tossed the stick he had been using to stoke the fire. "It has its advantages, being a shifter. Other than just flying around wherever I want."

"Such as?" Ryver stood and made her way to Cannon. His heart slammed against his ribs. His vision also went slightly blurry as she sat next to him. The rush of emotion for her was getting harder to ignore.

"Well, there's the strength, of course. The abilities to sense things that humans can't."

"Can you read minds?" Ryver lifted a hand and placed it over his. It was warm, soft, and glorious. Cannon breathed in deeply to keep himself together. "No, but I can catch people's scents easier. I can know what's coming before it gets too close."

Ryver smiled, then touched his face once again. He closed his eyes against it, falling deeper and deeper into her spell. She leaned in close, and he felt her breath, her scent, pouring over him like a soothing waterfall. "Did you see me coming?"

Cannon could no longer control himself. He decided it was pointless to resist. He touched her hand that was on his face and gave her a deep, sincere look. "I never saw you coming."

This time, Cannon pulled her body close to his, and he plunged in for a passionate kiss. She ran her hands through his hair and gripped his body tightly. He moved his hands all over her glorious ass, moving them upward toward her breasts. But he stopped and asked kindly. "Are you sure you want to do this?"

She nodded and bit his neck playfully. "More than anything."

TWELVE

RYVER

Ryver had been waiting for this moment ever since she first saw Cannon. His body was rippling with muscles but smooth and warm to her touch. His smile took her breath away. It was strange to feel so aroused in a situation where she should be worried about surviving, but it was a welcome break from the fear.

They kissed passionately, and she allowed herself to wander all over his body. She grabbed his hair, then moved down his bare shoulders, all the way to his torso, to just below his belt. She became wild as his powerful hands moved from her ass all the way up to her breasts, and she ached for him to touch her. But he leaned back just before touching them, asking her if this was what she wanted.

She nodded ferociously. "More than anything."

He smiled, then lifted her face by the chin. "It can be a little difficult with a human and shifter, but I will be careful with you. Just tell me if there's anything you don't like."

Ryver groaned. Being with him had made her body burn hotter than the Sahara desert in the middle of summer. "Don't worry," she stroked his face again. "I want you, Cannon."

They began kissing again, softly and slowly. His hands remained on her waist as they explored each other's mouth, tongues wandering in and out, touching lips and gliding over skin. Cannon kissed her from her lips to her cheeks, to her eyes, then moved down her neck. It was soft and delightful. Ryver closed her eyes and moaned. Cannon moved his mouth along her neck to her other shoulder, once again lightly marking her lovely skin. Ryver brought him back to her mouth, then gave him a long, slow kiss.

When she pulled away, he was smiling, his eyes gleaming. "I think you're wearing too many clothes," Ryver said and licked her lips.

Cannon looked down at himself, then stood. His shadow was huge in the firelight. Ryver laid herself down in front of him, keeping eye contact as she removed her pants and T-shirt. Cannon laid out his shirt and hers on the ground so she would be comfortable. As she lay on her back, Cannon gazed at her with concern. "Is that okay? The ground isn't exactly mattress-like."

Ryver nodded, her gaze all over his body. "It's fine."

Then she pulled him by the arm, so he lay on top of her. She remained in her bra and underwear, and he was still in his. She pressed her body against his tough and beautiful skin as they kissed in a warm embrace. She could feel his erection pushing against her through his underwear. The anticipation for his entry made her feel like her body was on fire.

Cannon sat back on his knees. He slowly removed Ryver's underwear, allowing her to lift her pelvis so he could slide them off her legs. He placed them aside with the rest of her clothes. His level of attention to her needs was spellbinding, but it only made her want him more. She knew he was holding back because of his strength, perhaps because he thought he might hurt her while in the throes of passion.

But she trusted him.

Cannon stopped for a moment and admired her body. She hadn't shaved in forever, not since she arrived to take care of the children, so self-consciousness filled her more than she thought she expected. Yet the look of pure adoration in his eyes made her feel like the most beautiful woman in the world. The fire flickered in front of them, casting shadows onto the cave – like the first stories ever told. He then lowered himself to move her upward. He did this tenderly with one hand on her lower back while the other moved to unclasp her bra. She loved his warmth, his delicious smell, as she pressed her lips into his chest. When her breasts were free, he admired them once again in silence.

"You are stunning."

Ryver watched his face soften and pure need fill his gaze. He stood to remove his own underwear, revealing a thick and large erection. Ryver knew that it wasn't the size of the tool but how you used it. But something about his thick and long penis stirred her loins more intensely.

She didn't realize it, but she let out an involuntary gasp at the sight of him. He laughed, then lowered himself down onto her. "I'll be careful with you. I would never hurt you, Ryver."

She thought he'd go straight for the main act, but instead he kissed his way down her body until it was obvious where he was headed. She lay back and gripped the clothes under her. He spread her legs wide, draping them over his bulging shoulders and lifting her ass off the ground and bringing it to his face. She thought maybe she should feel embarrassment or something like it. His face was inches from her sex. But no. All she knew was a rush of need travel through her like a shot of adrenaline.

"Let me taste you, Ryver." He groaned against her pussy. "You smell so good," he growled. "So delicious and I can't wait to eat you up."

She let out a soft moan the moment his tongue licked from her ass up to her clit. Her body immediately tensed and when he rubbed his face between her pussy folds she choked on a scream. The sensations of a quickly building climax caught her totally off guard. He didn't stop at her tense hold. Instead, he kissed and licked her pussy like a greedy beast. He sucked and groaned and fucked her with his tongue. Her whole body shuddered and it was only seconds later when he sucked hard at her clit that she came harder than she'd ever come in her life. She pressed her pussy to his mouth, her sex grasping at his tongue and dripping her essence all over his face. She forgot to breathe and then she realized she was holding her breath and let it out in a rush. All the while he was licking and lapping at her pussy, making her shudder.

"Fuck, sweetheart. You are even sweeter than I could have imagined."

She watched him lick his lips and crawl up to her to kiss her. The taste of her own release on his lips made her slick once more. She wasn't used to men doing anything like this. Sex in the past had been...so basic. This was explosive.

They kissed hard, rough and desperately. She relished in the touch of his naked body. His bare skin rubbed against hers. With the fire lighting up his beautiful features intermittently, Ryver already knew that this lovemaking was going to be the most romantic experience of her life.

They kissed as his dick moved against her body. She was slick and as ready as she was going to be for him after her orgasm, but he was big and she wasn't sure how it was going to feel. She wanted him inside her, but was a little apprehensive of his size. She wrapped her legs around him and fell deep into his touch, his kiss. They moaned together, learning more and more about how each other kissed and flaming the need between them.

Cannon broke the kiss and began moving down her body with his mouth. Again. Holy fuck. The man was on a mission. He moved from her neck to her breastbone, then finally began playing with her nipples. Ryver arched upward, cringing her face in the firelight.

"Oh, Cannon, yes."

He moved onto her other nipple then brought a wet finger to the opposite one. He played with both for a moment, controlling the electricity as it moved through her entire body. Slowly he kissed each breast, seeming to thank it, then moved down her belly, all the way to the crest of her center. Ryver raised her pelvis to his mouth. She wanted him so badly, and she swore she could feel pain in her opening.

"You want my mouth on your pussy again, love?"

She sucked in a hard breath and let it out softly. "Yes. God, yes."

Cannon grinned before moving his mouth to the center of her heat. He returned wistfully to her clit, then began teasing it with his tongue, lightly pressing against it. After the previous orgasm, she didn't think she'd be able to get so turned on so quickly. She was fucking wrong. Big time wrong. Tension wound slowly at her core. He sucked at her clit, licking down to her entrance and then shoving his tongue into her.

"Oh!"

Ryver thought her head was going to pop off. The things he was doing. No man had ever gone down on her in that way. It was as if he wanted to devour her and couldn't get enough of her taste. The grunts and groans were making her almost as turned on as his tongue flicking in and out of her pussy and up to her clit. None of the few guys she'd been with had ever considered that you had to lube up the engine before you got it running.

He sucked at her clit and moved his tongue in a circular motion. His head moved with it. Ryver began moving her hips slowly as if she was dancing. Cannon ran his fingers all over her, from the sides of her torso to the bottom of her ass. It was clear that he wanted her to feel the most pleasure she had ever experienced in her life.

"Oh, Cannon, oh, Cannon, I think I'm going to come again!"

She was on the edge of an intense orgasm. Even more than the first. She looked to the side of the cave and saw the silhouette of Cannon's strong back bent toward her – worshipping his goddess. This turned her on more than she thought possible.

Cannon brought his fingers to the tip of her opening, then slowly guided them into her wetness. She gasped at the sensation as he moved in and out, in and out. She worried a waterfall was going to stream out of her when she finally came. But instead of worrying about the results, she eased into it, closing her eyes and rhythmically moving against his strokes.

A volcano erupted inside her soon enough. It moved from the center of her stomach and sent shockwaves through her bones. It seemed to last over a minute – streams of pleasure taking her out of reality – and she shook with the aftershock.

"Oh fuck, oh my fucking God, Cannon!" Ryver lay with her arms over her face, breathing hard. She moaned and rocked back and forth. Cannon moved up her body with gentle kisses, eventually falling next to her, kissing her neck as she took in the moment.

"Holy shit, Cannon." She took her arms off her face then glanced down, realizing that Cannon was still completely erect. "You haven't even come yet."

Cannon chuckled. "I almost did, watching you. You're like a fucking piece of art, Ryver."

She quivered, reaching out to touch his face. "I want you inside me. Please."

Cannon kissed her. "I want that too, love."

THIRTEEN

CANNON

Cannon adored how badly Ryver wanted him. It was a different feeling to have someone desire you that completely. He had been shifter females, but he had never had this feeling. This feeling of knowing someone before you really knew them, especially when it came to sex. He had this need to be extra-gentle with her – a shifter's hunger could be a powerful thing not all humans would be able to take. He could easily hurt her if he lost control of himself and his desires.

He had experiences in the past where he had lost control and had hurt people he cared about. It was much easier to have an intense fuck session with another shifter because their strength and ability to absorb pain was at a higher threshold than humans.

So he went slow, despite Ryver's clear complaints. He was rock hard and knew that if he let himself go wild, he could potentially tear her and really injure her in this place where they weren't close to help. He wanted to make love to her, but he had to do it properly.

He grinned as he moved on top of her, not completely letting his weight fall. Her eyes blazed at him. "I have to go slow with this, and I don't want to hurt you."

She pulled him in closer, kissing him deeply. He wanted to let go entirely, to passionately lose himself in her. But he couldn't.

"I trust you, my big bad dragon."

And within that trust, he knew he could do no wrong.

On top of her, he placed the tip of his penis near the edge of her opening. He could feel her heart aching for him. He slowly moved inside her, paying close attention to her every movement. She bit the top of her lip and gazed up at him.

He raised his eyebrows. "Okay?"

She laughed, touching his face lovingly. "Yes, my love. You can keep going."

Love? Did she love him?

He moved inside her. She opened her legs wider so she could take him in. With long breaths, Cannon was able to get completely inside her and had to hold back from cumming instantly at the sensation of her tightness.

"Oh my god. I feel so full. So stretched." She smiled lovingly at him. "So perfect."

She grabbed him by the neck and encouraged him to begin stroking her. He did, but incredibly slowly, achingly slow. His eyes rolled back, and he moaned, feeling the inside of her. It triggered the dragon in him, the one that wanted to jackrabbit her pussy and have her scream his name. But he couldn't do that. Not yet anyway.

He gyrated inside her, and she breathed into his ear. Gradually, they fell into rhythm with one another, like ballet dancers moving to a quiet beat. Their breaths were hot and melodic, their moans succinct and tender. Cannon wanted to cum inside her, but that wasn't always something a woman would like or enjoy. He was getting close, but he wanted her to feel the ecstasy of his touch once more. It was the most beautiful sound echoing inside the cave.

"Ryver," he grunted, "I need to move. Please let me know if I am hurting you."

She smiled and kissed his lips. "You feel so incredible."

Her words riled him up, but he regained control and began moving ever so slightly faster inside her. She grunted but gripped his neck and back in pleasure rather than in pain. He continued on, feeling the rough portion of her G-spot, swelling and aching for him.

Ryver responded almost immediately to his increase in speed. "Oh, God. That feels amazing."

Cannon smiled and began kissing her neck as he moved inside her. She moaned his name over and over, pleading for him not to stop. Cannon wanted to send her to the moon with orgasms.

"Oh yes!" Ryver moved her hips hard against him again. She was soaking wet and completely taking him in. He slid in and out without hurting her but loving the sucking her pussy did on his cock every time he thrust in. He couldn't believe it in a way. His shifter nature made everything about him larger, bigger, more powerful.

She grabbed his head and spoke to him in a

hushed, aroused tone. "I'm gonna come again, oh my god..."

"That's it sweetheart. Come again. Over and over," Cannon whispered against her lips. As she did, Ryver's eyes rolled back, and she let out a high-pitched scream. Her body seized against him briefly, before she shook all over. Cannon held her close, grunting as his own orgasm reached its peak.

She nibbled on his ear. "Cum inside me, love. I want to feel you inside me."

Unable to think clearly, Cannon let himself go. He poured himself entirely into her center and roared her name. Ryver smiled and rocked against him, welcoming his seed inside her.

Cannon collapsed on top of her, still not entirely giving her his weight as he knew how tiny she was. His head spun – it had been a long time since he let go so freely. A wave of dizziness shook him, so he rolled off her then stared at her with awe. She was pure magic.

"Ryver," he said breathlessly. "You're so beautiful."

Ryver leaned onto her side, also breathless and sweating. "You're not so bad yourself, my big bad dragon."

She inched closer to him, leaning her head

on his chest. His heart was pounding, not only from the orgasm but from the emotions jetting through his mind and soul. He'd never emotions like these about anyone, and she had called him *her love*. He wasn't sure if she had meant that the same way he did, but he wasn't going to ruin the moment by asking.

Cannon stroked her hair and breathed in her scent. Her vagina tasted like fresh dew. He swore he could live between her legs forever.

But what of his freedom? The desire to live on the mountain alone? Ryver had completely discombobulated his original plan. And now that he had slept with the subject, what would that mean about the deal he had made?

His mind was swirling, but Ryver eased it. She lifted her head and kissed him, mixing her tongue with her own juices. She pulled back and leaned her chin on his chest.

"So that's what it's like to be with a shifter."

Cannon laughed. "Yep, what would the rating be?"

Without hesitation, Ryver said, "Oh, eleven out of ten definitely."

"Have you never been with a shifter?"

Ryver shook her head. Cannon had figured this but wasn't going to assume.

"I had two boyfriends in college and one in med school, but the sex was nothing like this."

Cannon was glowing. "I hope that's a good thing."

Ryver tapped one of his pecs lightly. "Of course, it's a good thing! I've never come twice with anyone other than myself."

"Well," Cannon sat up, taking her face in his. "That's something we can change."

Ryver smiled, her cheeks growing rosy. "Where the hell did you come from, Cannon?"

"Oh, some hole in the wall down south, I think."

She lay back on his chest. "Honestly?"

"No, but that's a story for another time. Now I think we have to wash up again in that chilly river."

Ryver pointed at the fire. "As long as we've got that, I think we're good to go."

"So that means it's your turn to get firewood?"

Ryver gave a soft throaty laugh, and it was the most delightful sound. Cannon thought about telling her that he was pretty sure he loved her, that he knew she was his mate, but he couldn't summon the courage. Instead, he kissed her forehead and began rubbing her chest.

"You're beautiful, Ryver."

"You already said that," Ryver joked.

"I think I'm going to be saying it forever, so get used to it."

They both laughed in each other's arms, the firelight continuing to flicker and light up their features in the dark.

Cannon didn't know what the future held, but all he knew was that his plans had changed drastically when this woman had fallen out of the sky and into his life.

FOURTEEN

RYVER

Ryver eventually took Cannon's advice and had a dip in the stream again. She was sweaty and dripping with his wetness, and she didn't want to fall asleep that way. She stood in the river completely naked, feeling the cool air pass over her skin. She closed her eyes as she threw water onto herself. No one had ever made her feel this way, sexually or sentimentally. She knew she was still radiating from her multiple orgasms, but there was something real about her time with Cannon that seemed raw and meaningful.

The majority of the time she had spent with men was professional. Adam and Luke McKay, for example, were male doctors that she spent the most time with, even before being shipped off to help children. Ryver interacted with them platonically and had no real desire to go beyond anything but that. She wouldn't do anything with anyone within the boundaries of work anyway – that would just be stupid.

Her father had taught her that you don't shit where you eat.

She had only shared her body and mind with three other men, and it had been years since then. The last being in med school. Daniel had been his name. She initially thought he had a cute smile and laugh. He'd tried to get her to quit med school to marry him and become his trophy wife with no life. She broke it off and hadn't been sexual with anyone since. It sounded like a long time in her mind as she ruminated by the river, but she knew how to take care of herself in that way without a man's help. In the whole year that she and Daniel had dated, she had only three real orgasms. And before him only two other times.

The others she had faked, merely to get the experience over with so she could get the job done herself. She thought maybe she'd built up the idea of sex in her mind and that this was the actual reality of it, something that was overblown entirely and merely an average experience.

But that didn't feel like the case with Cannon. He genuinely wanted her to feel good, which was a foreign feeling for Ryver. She did everything she could to embrace that as they made love. Even when he was being so gentle with her, it was almost irritating.

But she hadn't ever been with a shifter, so perhaps it would have been dangerous for him to go all out.

Oh well, maybe next time.

Ryver got dressed by the stream then returned to the cave. Cannon was lying near the fire he had rebuilt, the flame flicking high in the small space. He was only wearing his underwear and looked like he was posing for her.

"Well, that's a nice sight," Ryver said, walking up to him and kissing him deeply. She lay next to him and faced him, his features dancing in the light.

He grinned. "Look who's talking, beautiful."

Ryver sarcastically rolled her eyes. "You really weren't kidding about that, eh?"

Cannon shook his head. "You'll find that I rarely kid about anything."

Ryver laughed, then lay on her hands.

"You know, I've never had multiple orgasms like that."

Cannon raised his eyebrows. "What?"

Ryver nodded. "Yep. First time for everything, I guess."

"I only counted two." Cannon grinned.

"That's more than I'm used to!"

Ryver told him more about her former lover, and Cannon couldn't help but laugh.

"Well, he clearly didn't know what he was doing. And he also missed out on an entire treasure trove of experiences with you."

Ryver could feel herself blushing. She hid her face in her hands. How was she feeling like this right now? When she should be focusing on not being murdered?

What a surreal turn of events, she thought to herself.

She was exhausted, pleasantly, every cell in her body still humming from their lovemaking. But she knew she wasn't going to be able to sleep. She peered at Cannon for a long moment.

"What?" he said, still smiling.

"Who are you, really?"

Cannon pursued his lips. "That's an incredibly long story that would be best told when we're both not exhausted."

Ryver shook her head. "I'm tired, but I'm too excited to sleep. I want to know everything about you." She reached out and stroked his face. He smiled and kissed her hand. They lowered their hands down together, still embraced.

"Well," Cannon stated, rubbing a hand over the back of his neck.

"Oh, yeah," she blurted. "What is that on your neck? I felt it when we were..." Her face flushed red hot, cheeks melting off. When Cannon didn't reply, she noticed he was scowling. "Hey, I didn't mean to be nosey. If it's personal..."

"No," he answered and blew out a breath, "Ryver, I can't lie to you." He paused, then took a deep breath. "I've been in a shifter prison for the past couple of years."

Her mind blanked. The words didn't make sense. He was a good, caring guy. "What do you mean?"

His brows drew down. "I'm a criminal. According to the U.S. government, anyway. I was arrested and thrown into prison. This implant in my neck kept me from being able to shift."

She snatched her hand back then immediately regretted it. "What did you do?"

"A group of shifters decided that they'd had enough of being suppressed and rallied for their civil rights. As you can imagine, things got out of control, and a riot broke out. I happened to be on the wrong side of the line."

She scoffed. "But a peaceful gathering is your right to do."

"Apparently, not shifters' right. Because I'm a dragon shifter, I can fly off anywhere. So I have been everywhere, and no matter where I went, shifters were discriminated against. There are so many countries that think shifters are a menace to society and that they only want to take over and kill all humans."

Ryver nodded, horrified by what she was hearing.

Cannon continued. "But in my experience, I've found that's rarely the case. You are going to find malevolent people – or shifters – in many places, but most shifters I've interacted with just want to live their lives. Simple as that."

Ryver smiled. "That's all anybody can want."

Cannon suddenly seemed embarrassed, his

cheeks turning a rosy red in the darkness. "I honestly don't think I've spoken this much in years."

"I'm glad it's to me." Ryver moved closer, laying her head against his chest. "So you help shifters in their quests?"

"It's mostly to keep them from being captured. Many governments like to take them in on phony charges with very little evidence being obtained, then expose them to groups of people who already have a prejudice against us. So yeah, I think I try to help them be free."

"So they let you out to get me?"

There was a beat of silence, and Ryver instantly regretted asking. She assumed "they" had offered him a sweet deal to come out and save her. But they definitely did not send him to fall in love with her.

"In a way, yes. Freedom is something we all crave, isn't it?"

Ryver nodded against his chest. Her eyes were getting heavy, loving the low rumble of his voice as it sounded in his chest. She wanted to know so much more, but she was going to doze off any second.

"How did they capture you?" Ryver yawned

once again. Cannon laughed and lay his head next to her.

"Let's talk about that later. You need to rest, beautiful."

Ryver was ready to question him vehemently, but she dozed off fast, warm and relaxed by the fire and her new lover.

After a few hours, Ryver awoke to a strange sensation. It took her a minute to refocus her eyes in the darkness, as the fire had gone out as they slept. It was a light tickling on her leg that could have been the wind. But when she looked down, the reality was something much more insidious.

On her thigh was a scorpion, crawling around without concern. It was the size of her fist. She didn't think it had noticed that she had awoken, but she wasn't going to take any more chances with a dangerous animal.

FIFTEEN

RYVER

Cannon woke to Ryver's voice calling his name. She noticed it took him a few seconds to notice she wasn't saying it sweetly but with terror. He opened his eyes and sat up. She was pointing at something in the dark.

"We have a visitor," she whispered.

The scorpion waddled about on her leg, flicking its stinger in the air as if it were a threat. Ryver sat still, hoping it wouldn't notice they were both staring down at it.

"Don't move," Cannon said quietly.

Cannon looked down and saw the large scorpion making a home on her leg. In a blurring motion, he rolled away from her, grabbing a nearby stick. He flicked it off her leg, which clearly startled it. Before it could scurry away, he smashed it hard with a rock. They both heard the intense crunching sound of its skeleton turning to dust.

"Jesus Christ!" Ryver said through laughter. "That scared the shit out of me!"

"No wonder," Cannon said as he lifted the rock to inspect what he'd done. "These are the deadly kind, so you don't want to take any chances with that."

"Fuck." Ryver stood quickly, looking around to see if she could find any more. In that second, everything she'd been through in the last several days came crashing around her. Cannon embraced her, and her heart sped a mile a minute.

She was frustrated and angry. All she wanted to do was get somewhere safe with Cannon where they could live their lives together.

"It's okay. There's no way you would have known that."

She held back tears, pressing her face into his chest. "It feels like I'm at death's door at every turn around here!" She yelled, expressing a feeling she had been holding back for some time. It was like a fairy tale being with Cannon out here. But no matter how lovely being with him was, there was a terrible world waiting for her outside. But what could she do about it?

Cannon stroked her hair and her back. She was tiny and almost had her face in his waist. He bent over slightly to accommodate the difference and reassured her that everything was okay. It made her heart swoon.

"They normally don't come up this high, so that guy was probably lost. It was just a freak occurrence."

"Those seem to happen a lot around here."

Ryver found it hard to be vulnerable, so she tried to lean into the moment and listen to his words without feeling defensive. But that was her nature, and she could feel her anxiety and anger swelling inside like a red-hot balloon.

"We are safe right now," Cannon said. "We will head out when it gets dark again, and we will make sure we look out for each other."

Ryver looked up at him, tears in her eyes. She wiped them and smiled. Her anxiety was beginning to fade. She truly believed him when he spoke, and that was all she really needed to hear.

"Thank you. I'm sorry, that really took a lot out of me."

"No need to apologize." He had his hands

on her shoulders. "You can sleep on top of me if you want. No scorpions will get past me."

Ryver smiled, then hugged him close. She knew safety in his arms. Fear dissipated whenever he was near.

Ryver sat, having calmed down. Cannon lit another fire as they were both slightly chilly. Cannon put his clothes on and wrapped his arms around her. She shivered slightly, so he brought out the warmth of his dragon. He really was like a human furnace.

She snuggled into him. "Thank you," she whispered again.

Despite the scorpion scare, Cannon fell asleep quickly. Ryver held him and tried to stop thinking about the possible enemies outside waiting for them. She thought about their future and what things might look like when they got out of this mess. But this wasn't real life – it was like chewing on a bite of candy and letting yourself absorb the taste. The rest of life was the distinct indifferent flavor she hadn't realized she had grown accustomed to.

But what if it didn't have to be that way anymore?

He was a mercenary, yes, in a world that

Ryver had never considered. But he defied those stereotypes and anything she had ever imagined before. He was arrested on bogus charges, it sounded like. She wouldn't hold that against him.

She fell asleep in his arms, imagining their life away from fear and the potential for violence.

He awoke before she had when night had fallen. She saw him packing their things away as she sat up.

"Good evening, sweet Ryver," Cannon said.

Ryver smiled. She knew this wasn't going to be an easy night. She wished they could continue talking in this cave, getting to know each other, and just living in the eternal bliss of their bodies and souls. But they had to get out of there – who knew how long it would take until another group would find them?

He held her for a moment as if he had sensed her fears. He was good at that – maybe it was a shifter thing. He kissed her forehead and glanced down at her. "You good to go?"

She shrugged. "I'm as ready as I'll ever be."

He slipped his backpack on and offered her a hand up. She stood stronger than she had anticipated. She followed Cannon, and he reached out his hand for her. She smiled and took it. He led her out of the cave into the darkness. He removed a flashlight from his pocket, and they went down the path.

A thought occurred. "Cannon, I've seen you shift, but that thing in your neck..."

"When I agreed to their plans, they replaced the original implant with one that lets me partially shift so I could get you."

"What purpose does that serve?" she asked. He shrugged. "That's inhumane. It's not right. Why do they want you so bad?" she whispered.

"Fear," he simply answered.

Ryver scoffed. "I feel like it must be more by the amount of effort they are putting into it."

Cannon continued along the path, leading them with the flashlight. "The prison is slowly starting to become known. Maybe the public will oppose it as I do."

That was something Ryver hadn't thought of. Perhaps she could bring attention to their plight. Or to at least expose it to the world. Ryver knew this was how Cannon felt, and she started to believe many people all over the world would have a problem with this.

Those in power had taken away these shifters' freedom.

They continued to walk through the night, stopping only to take on water and have a snack or two. The protein bars were keeping her full, but she was definitely going to need a real meal soon. Her clothes got bigger, day by day – and not in a way that she wanted.

They arrived at an area of thick brush. Cannon took Ryver by the hand and led them both through. Ryver could barely see, but she trusted Cannon. He used his flashlight in his other hand, both to show them the way and to push away branches. Below them was damp dirt, squishing underneath their boots. It was cramped, so they moved slowly.

"There's a branch here right at your level. Watch out."

When branches would pull back against Cannon's body, he would warn Ryver before pushing past it. She would raise a hand and block it. She was thankful for the few times a small branch nearly slapped her in the face.

"Thanks for that." Ryver giggled as she pushed through the brush. Just as she was stepping over a thick log, she heard a sound that caught her completely off guard. She stopped moving completely.

"Cannon, wait a minute," she whispered. He stopped, then turned back to her, still holding branches.

"What is it?"

Ryver held up her finger to her lips to keep Cannon from talking. She heard the sound again. It was high-pitched. "I think a baby is crying out there."

SIXTEEN

CANNON

Cannon stood in the middle of the brush, not knowing what to think of what he was hearing. He listened intently again and did think that it sounded like a baby crying. But he feared it might be a setup – getting to Ryver was seeming like a priority for many people these days.

"Ryver, it might be a trap."

The crying sounded off again, and it was slightly ahead of them and to the left. If they kept going straight, they would surely pass it. Ryver pulled at his hand as he walked forward.

"I know," she groaned. "But if it's not? We can't just leave it!" she whisper-shouted at him. He didn't want to leave it either in case it actually was a child in the forest. How the hell did a baby get all the way out here anyway?

Cannon pulled back at her hand and whispered back to her. "We have to be careful. Let's go slow, just in case." He could tell Ryver was concerned, and he was as well. But their lives were on the line, and they had to treat every moment like it mattered.

Cannon moved slightly to the left to follow the cry. He continued to step lightly, squishing into the wet dirt. He wanted to feel around for landmines in case the cry was just a recording. He had seen traps that took advantage of the kindness of people's hearts. If he found a mine, he could let it explode in his dragon form, and he could survive it.

It took them almost half an hour to get even close to the sound. Cannon saw Ryver itching to move ahead faster. He held her back, reminding her that they needed to be careful. She huffed at him, but he understood the sentiment.

They finally arrived at where the baby's cries were coming from. There was a small clearing, and Cannon was able to make out outlines lying on the ground. One was much larger than the other. The tiny one was moving under a covering. He continued to walk slowly and carefully in a systematic pattern surrounding the baby. When he had cleared the area, he motioned for Ryver to step forward.

She nearly ran to the baby's side. "It *is* a baby! Cannon, it's a baby!"

He came to her side and pushed the blanket aside. It indeed was a male infant, arms and legs flailing in the air. The shape beside him was his mother, who had been shot and left for dead. Cannon winced at the sight of her.

"Jesus Christ." Cannon touched the baby's face. He was cold and probably hungry. "Here, pick him up for me."

Ryver lifted him with ease, wrapping up the baby. The child continued to cry. Cannon placed his hand over the child's forehead. Ryver watched in astonishment as the baby's cries turned to whimpers, then quickly fell into a restful slumber.

Cannon's inner warmth move through his fingers and into the baby. He was glad the babe was able to rest.

Ryver stared in amazement. "What the hell was that?" she whispered.

"I told you, I'm a human furnace." Cannon winked. "You don't get to be a dragon without using your warmth every now and then."

Ryver grinned, then held the baby against her chest. A look of concern flashed over her face.

"What are we going to do? We can't leave him here."

Cannon shook his head. He knew this was going to slow them down, but there was no way he was leaving a child out here to die. There was probably a village nearby they could leave the child, so it was safe.

"We aren't going to leave him. I have an idea about where we can take him. Come."

Cannon held Ryver by one hand while she held the baby in her other. They still had to move through thick brush, but it was increasingly more difficult with a tiny baby with them. Cannon softly pushed the branches out of the way, holding them so Ryver could step past them. They arrived at a village after an hour of straining through the brush.

Cannon was thankful for the break in the thick vegetation so he could stretch his long limbs. They stepped quietly through the dark, trying not to alert anyone. Everyone seemed to be asleep, so that worked for them.

They both crouched in the bush, looking over a small hut nearby. "Here's the plan – We're going to place him on that doorstep, and someone is going to take him in."

Ryver looked down at the baby. He knew she had attached herself to him, even though their interaction was brief. It was difficult not to connect with someone through hardship, even if that someone was a baby.

But she agreed it was the best course of action. She kissed the baby's head and passed him to Cannon. The infant was still breathing lightly and asleep. Cannon held him in his big hands and wrapped him tightly in the blanket. "Good luck, little guy," he said before leaving Ryver by the bush.

He crept in the dark to the door of the hut. He lay the baby down softly, making sure to rest its head on some leaves found nearby. He lifted a fist and let it hover on the door. He looked at Ryver, who was ready to flee. He knocked loudly, then fled back to the bush with Ryver.

The two stood behind the bush and watched as a light came on in the hut. Someone came to the door, a woman gasped at the sight of the baby. She looked around, afraid, then picked up the baby. She called out to anyone who might be nearby then hastily went inside. Ryver sighed with relief.

Cannon placed a hand on her shoulder. "He'll be okay. We did the right thing."

Ryver kissed him quickly. "Thank you."

Surprised and delighted by the kiss, Cannon smiled. "You have to stop thanking me, and I'm not the one doing all the work here."

She smiled back, then allowed him to lead her back into the forest.

They had returned to their original pathway, pushing through in the dark, when Ryver whispered, "You were really good with that baby. Do you have kids?"

Cannon kept moving through the brush. "No, I never had the chance."

"Hey, Cannon," They stopped in the middle of the thick brush. "Can we rest for a second?"

Cannon could sense the sunrise approaching, and he wanted to keep going. But she wasn't a shifter, so she was probably greatly fatigued.

He stopped and leaned back against a tree. Ryver came toward him, taking him by both hands. "That was really scary."

"You mean with the baby?"

"Well, yeah, the baby and the mother. Seeing death like that is terrifying."

It hadn't occurred to Cannon that Ryver

wasn't as accustomed to violence as he was. Seeing the dead mother had still affected him, but it wasn't something he carried with him. Years of seeing people die had made him desensitized.

He held her hands and kissed them. "You're right," he whispered. "It's a good thing we came across him."

"What do you think happened?" Ryver asked.

Cannon sighed. "It could have been any of the militias around here, to be honest. They seem willing to kill anyone to get what they want."

Cannon knew this was going to rile up Ryver's anxiety, so he pulled her to him. "But we're getting close, and I promise you, we will be fine."

He knew he shouldn't make promises like that. If things weren't working out this way in human form, then he would shift into his dragon and run off with her, whether she liked it or not.

He would keep that to himself.

A strange scent floated on the wind. Before he could react, a gun barrel poked him in the back. In the native language, he heard, "Don't move, or I'll shoot you."

SEVENTEEN

RYVER

Ryver gasped when she heard the rough voice behind Cannon. She pulled back to see a man in village clothing holding a gun aimed at them. Cannon slowly raised his hands and spoke in the tongue of the villagers.

Was this the person who shot the mother and left the baby to die? Anger and fear seared through her, but she trusted Cannon to keep her safe. That thought surprised her. He was the first man she'd ever truly believed in.

Cannon continued talking and the tension in the air dissipated as the gun lowered. After a moment, he gave the man a nod, and the man smiled, saying something then walking away.

"What the hell was that about?" she asked, nearly breathless with the turn of events.

"He's on night patrol from the village. When the mother and child didn't return home, some of the men went out to search. In doing so, they came across a new militia group east of here. He warned us to go south."

"That was nice of him."

Cannon grunted. "He told us and didn't shoot first because he saw us return the child to the village. I told him where he could find the mother."

"Oh. Glad to help."

"Me too," he said.

The night continued, but time stayed strained through velvet. Ryver stopped looking skyward to get an idea of time. It only made her depressed. Every step was fraught as they dared not let their guard down and surged forward without knowing if they were walking into the hands of armed men.

Hours passed, and Ryver resigned herself to walking forever in this purgatory of darkness and danger. Strangely, she almost became numb to it when Cannon pulled on her sleeve.

"Hey, daydreamer. Look," he said, pointing up.

Once again, she followed his finger and saw that the inky black was giving way to the morning light. Ribbons of lilac, saffron, and tangerine competed for attention above her. Were she not so tired, she would have cried at the beauty.

"Dealer's choice. I smell chimney smoke ahead, which means a village is nearby. Do you want to stop here or keep going?"

Ryver wondered at Cannon giving her responsibility for making this choice. But she also knew he wouldn't steer her deliberately into danger.

"We could see if a room could be rented. I have money in my pack," Cannon continued. "But I understand if we're both... hesitant."

The thought of water even a measure above freezing and perhaps even a real bed floated in her mind, insistent and inviting.

"Let's keep moving. At least to check it out. If we get a good feeling, we'll proceed. If not, the earth is our bed."

Cannon smiled. "A good plan."

They continued, and sure enough, Ryver soon saw the same smoke trails. They saw a clutch of huts arrayed in a protective ring through the curtain of trees. A small village, that was certain, but Ryver could only hope that someone had a room to offer.

With silent nods to each other, Cannon and

Ryver walked into the village, holding their hands at their sides to indicate they carried nothing of harm and that they came in peace.

At first, Ryver worried they would be run out of the village or worse. Cautious eyes peered out of doorways, and those sweeping their front steps or doing their morning chores paused to look.

The houses clustered around a central square, and it was here that Cannon and Ryver paused to get their bearings.

"It's okay. They just need to see we won't do them any harm," Cannon said from the side of his mouth as they looked around. He spoke out in another language.

"Morning," Ryver called to a woman who stood nearby. To her surprise, the woman waved back.

A small knot of villagers conferred with each other. Ryver tried not to let her anxiety show. Finally, a woman, the same one who waved, approached.

"Welcome," she said. Ryver was shocked that the woman spoke English. Her hair was tied in a kerchief. Her face was ruddy and fresh but, as Ryver looked more closely, she saw crow's feet and laugh lines deeply etched in her skin.

A woman who enjoyed life, or at least a good laugh, Ryver thought.

"Thank you. We are not dangerous," Ryver said, trying to keep the tone light.

"That seems obvious," the woman replied. "We are small in number, but we like to think we can be welcoming."

"So far, I agree with you," Ryver said, her anxiety tapering a little.

"You are not tourists. That much is clear."

Cannon stepped closer. "That is true. We are trying to avoid... the trouble that is working north of here."

The woman's face darkened with sadness. "Yes, it is unfortunate. And not who we are. We thought the troubles would not reach this far, but we were wrong."

"Is there anyone here who would be willing to rent us a room? Only for a few hours. We just need sleep. The night has been... long," Ryver said, recalling the past few hours with a shudder.

Cannon again interjected, opening his palm to show the woman. "We have money."

The woman looked at the bills folded in Cannon's hand, and Ryver noted how her eyes lit up. "American money! My name is Wentra. I can spare a room. Follow me."

Ryver tried to disguise her palpable relief at the offer. Nodding, they followed the woman. She turned, shooting a look at the other villagers as if to say, "all is well here."

Wentra led the pair to a squat house tucked behind the main houses on the square. Though simple and plain, it was clean and warm.

They entered into a sitting room/kitchen where a fire blazed. A handful of other rooms peeked off from the main room in other directions. Ryver immediately saw the foot of a wooden bed with fresh linens just off to the right.

It looked almost too good to be true.

"Your room will be through there. I'll make you some eggs if you like. Towels are on the shelf behind the door."

They both thanked her profusely, and Cannon placed the wad of bills on the worn but well-loved kitchen table. Wentra, with one quick motion, picked them up and secreted them in her pocket.

Then she set about cooking a simple but delicious breakfast. As the smell permeated the kitchen, Ryver salivated.

After a wash and a meal, Ryver was a new woman.

"You can rest now. You will not be disturbed," Wentra said over her shoulder as she cleaned the dirty dishes.

Ryver didn't need to be told twice. Already she could feel the exhaustion of a long night, and a full belly start to pull her down into sleep.

They retreated to their room and pulled off their outer clothes.

"Can we trust them?" Ryver whispered. She wanted to believe that Wentra was a woman of her word, but the antics of the farmer that had betrayed them were not easily forgotten.

"I think so. They are scared of these military groups in a way the farmer wasn't. I also sense a pride here. A pride that helps us." Cannon replied thoughtfully.

"But she took our money," Ryver countered.

"True. But she must trust us."

"And why's that?"

"We're the good guys," Cannon said without missing a beat.

By now, Ryver had pulled back the thick covers of the blanket. The clean sheets beckoned to her like a siren song. Even if Wentra betrayed them now, Ryver might not care. She was too tired.

Trusting in Cannon's words, she was soon asleep.

Once again, it was not long enough. Consciousness was once upon her. But this time, she could not speak.

Cannon's hand was covering her mouth.

EIGHTEEN

CANNON

It was harder than usual to wake Ryver. That wasn't surprising, given how much he had struggled to wake.

He noted the time. The afternoon was fading to early evening. They had slept the day away. Still, she refused to wake. He could see why Ryver was sluggish. The long, difficult days and her injuries were catching up to her. But it was imperative that she woke and that they stay quiet.

Finally, after nudging her one more time, a little rougher than he'd like, her body shifted, her eyes fluttered and opened. Her mouth widened as if about to speak, and Cannon clamped his hand over it. When he did, her eyes widened in alarm.

"Shhh," he whispered, trying to sound calm.

He knew he was sending mixed signals but could only hope she'd forgive him.

"We have to stay quiet, and we have to leave. Now. I'll explain soon. I'm sorry."

The fear didn't leave her eyes, but he saw in the light of the lengthening shadows that filtered through the room's only window that she understood his urgency. She nodded in comprehension.

He was glad to release his hand. In near silence, they dressed and gathered their few belongings. His body ached for more sleep and more time next to her warm body, but danger compelled them to be on their way. The very air around them was laden with tension. The once-friendly village became hostile and unwelcome. They had to move on.

Once packed, they opened their bedroom door a crack, scanning the sitting room beyond for Wentra. Cannon dared not leave before checking in with her.

Like a specter, she appeared from the corner. Apparently, she had been keeping watch at the front window.

"Thank goodness. I was worried you would not hurry. Leave by the back door. My friend Hisr will lead you the back way out of the village. From there, you can disappear into the forest. Stick to the shadows." She spoke in a hushed whisper.

"How can we thank you?" Cannon began, but Wentra held up her hand.

"No need. You paid me, didn't you? And I have a good feeling about you. Before I forget, take this." She handed a small bundle to him. From the sounds within and the weight, Cannon surmised it was food and water.

Gratefully accepting it, he nodded his thanks one more time. Ryver clasped Wentra's hands in silent appreciation, and they left the house by the back door.

Sure enough, a thin man dressed all in black with a woolen cap emerged from the growing shadows just behind Wentra's house.

"You must be Hisr," Cannon said.

In response, Hisr merely nodded and gestured they were to follow him in single file and stay as close as possible.

Eyes darting and all senses on high alert, Cannon followed Hisr, and Ryver brought up the rear. They skirted behind a small garden and through two more small houses before the edge of the village loomed. The forest lay just beyond a patch of ground that looked to be a fallow field.

When they reached its edge, Hisr stopped. With a furtive glance to check they were alone, he finally spoke. His voice was low and clipped. His whole body was tense.

"This is where I leave you. Run as fast as you can. You are exposed there. Forest is beyond. Follow the tree line."

Cannon surveyed their path. It was true. The field was exposed, but night's shadows were growing. Anyone running across it would be an easy target if someone happened to be looking for them. But the safe density of the forest beckoned. They had to risk it.

He knew they couldn't stay in the village. Nor could he continue to risk the lives of Hisr and Wentra.

"Thank you," Cannon said.

Hisr barely nodded and turned on his heel. A second later, he was gone, having melted into the advancing night.

Cannon gave one encouraging look to Ryver, who responded with a look of dogged determination. They bent low and ran in a crouch as fast as they could across the patch of open ground. A few stray birds, their only witnesses.

A great feeling of relief washed over him when

they reached the first line of trees without incident. Still, he dared not speak until they were well within the forest. The tree line snaked up in a jagged path to the left. They followed it.

"What happened back there?" Ryver asked, breaking the silence when they were well on their way.

"Wentra woke me. The militia had arrived and was going house to house, taking food and other things. Wentra said it was the price for the village's protection."

"Oh," Ryver said, wonder in her voice.

"Yes. And, as you know, there is hardship here. Wentra knew it wouldn't take much for someone to cave. I am grateful to her."

"As am I," Ryver said thoughtfully.

"You chose well," Cannon observed.

"Me? What did I choose?"

"You spoke to her first. You must have had a good feeling about her."

They walked a few paces in silence as Ryver chewed on his words.

"I'm not sure about that. She just seemed friendly to me," she said finally.

"Well, whatever it was, I'm happy you did.

That was a small village. They were going to find us any minute."

"I hope those people don't suffer because of us."

"As do I. But if anyone did sell us out, I would understand. They are being tested. They are tired, hungry, and people do strange things when they are like that for too long."

With an astonished look on her face, Ryver turned to Cannon.

"You would understand? After what that farmer did to us?"

Now it was time for Cannon to consider her words. "You're right. But somehow, I knew Wentra wouldn't do that to us."

Night was falling rapidly now. This part of the forest was denser than the one from the night before but, from all appearances, was without human life. Which meant they could walk relatively worry free.

"So, what's it to be? Care for a walk in the woods?" Cannon asked.

Ryver laughed, and Cannon was cheered by the sound. It resembled water dropping on glass.

"Do I have a choice?" she said, playfully swatting at him.

"I suppose. What's it to be?"

Ryver looked up. The stars were just starting to peek out from the fading azure of the sky. Soon, they would need his night vision once more.

"We should keep moving. The bad guys are never far behind," she said with resignation.

"How's your side?"

"Better. Sleep helps."

"When this is over, we shall sleep well. I promise."

Ryver stopped walking and looked directly at Cannon.

"I truly hope so. Wentra's bed was downright luxurious."

Cannon chuckled. "Trust me. After what I slept on in prison, I agree with you."

Ryver leaned forward and gave him a kiss. Desire flooded through him, but he also knew a deep sense of calm, of belonging. Somehow, against all odds, she brought that out in him. He had to protect her at all costs.

And not because it was his job.

"Let's keep walking," he proposed.

"Do we know where we are headed?"

"To the most comfortable bed in the world," he replied, kissing her on the forehead.

She laughed and swatted at him once more.

"Well, why didn't you say so? Lead the way!"

Cannon gave both her hands a little squeeze and started walking. Sounds of night creatures welled up from the now hidden crannies of the trees and fallen logs. Within a few minutes, darkness would overtake them – a comfort and a liability both at the same time.

He led the way, his night vision ticking up as the minutes clicked by. The terrain was uneven, and it even rose a little like they were walking up a small hill. Ryver, he could tell, was lost in her thoughts. He let her remain there as he needed his concentration to ensure the path ahead was clear of bandits.

His keen senses told him the area was different than what they had previously encountered. It was murkier with a swampy quality. The air smelled more pungent here – the smell of decomposing plants and standing water.

He stepped around a particularly mushy spot, pushing away thick brambles. They had walked at least a mile when Cannon noticed the air was much thicker and that the night insects were plentiful. But it was the Congo jungle. He was glad it was not a hot night, or things would be much worse.

From a short distance behind him, he heard a squeak. Turning to ask Ryver how she was doing, Cannon was met with a shock. Instead of seeing her, he was alone. Where was she?

NINETEEN

RYVER

It had been creeping up on her, but now, there was no denying it. At first, she just thought she could power through it, ignore the deadening weight that pulled at her muscles and tendons and ligaments.

But it pushed back, invading her mind, making her brain slow. Her thoughts became one-note, fixated only on one thing: she needed to sleep.

The past couple of days, the lack of reliable sleep and nourishing food and her injuries were becoming too much for her body to handle. The rest at Wentra's was welcome, but any benefits she had gained from it were long used up.

Cannon seemed unstoppable, and she did not want to be a burden on him. Every ounce of her energy was focused on walking forward, making good progress, and listening for any sign that someone who wanted them dead or captured was near.

So, she kept silent, lifting her feet in agonizing rhythm, hoping that soon, perhaps, they could stop. But she willed her voice to stay silent. She would not whine or complain.

This was where she found herself when the sinkhole appeared. Had she been more alert, she might have seen it and stepped to the side, avoiding it altogether. But, in her haze and exhaustion, she let her foot sink right in. She tried to scream for Cannon, but only a squeal came out.

In the process of walking, her momentum carried her forward almost face-first into the quagmire. Her hands shot out, trying to catch her, but there was no solid ground to break her fall, and she plunged full-body into the faux concrete.

As panic overtook her, the sinkhole, like a snake, swallowed her more. The tight embrace of the mud was upon her, squeezing out her very life's breath. Adrenaline shot through her.

She tried to calm herself, but the surrounding muck and mire closed in on her like a coffin. Then, she spied movement in the gloom just beyond.

Though it had only been a second, it could have been forever. But Cannon had mercifully noticed she was no longer behind him and had returned to find her rapidly sinking.

"Stay calm, just stay calm. I will get you out of here. If you thrash or panic, you will sink faster," he said, his voice soothing but direct. She blinked rapidly to show she understood, but her field of vision grew hazy as her oxygen levels dropped.

Ryver had always had a healthy respect for fear and danger. She would never call herself weak or timid, but she knew where her comfort zone lay, and she never strayed much beyond it.

Now, here she was, slowly being entombed in sludge and trying to force herself to feel a sense of calm. But how could she? One of her greatest fears was coming true – being buried alive.

To make matters worse, Cannon suddenly disappeared. Every ounce of her being nearly gave up entirely. She wanted to scream for him to come back, to not leave her like this. However, moments later, he returned with a thick branch in his hands.

Standing near the edge of the sinkhole, Cannon called out, clearly and succinctly. "Grab this and hold on as tight as you can. I will pull you out."

Like the closing of an oculus, her vision was beginning to narrow and weaken.

"Grab it, Ryver. For me," he said, and something within her gathered the strength needed to activate her hands. Trembling and weak, they sought and found the rough bark of the branch and clung like a vise.

Cannon pulled. An ordinary man might have been defeated by the pull of the sinkhole. But Cannon, bracing his feet against a rock that ringed the sinkhole edge, pulled Ryver up a foot, freeing her chest.

Sweet, precious air filled her lungs, and the looming darkness in her eyes retreated. He pulled once more, and her lower half was freed. The sinkhole reset itself with a final protesting slurp, waiting for its next victim.

As she emerged from the muck, her whole body seemed to collapse in on itself. Crumpling at the sinkhole's edge, Cannon let her catch her breath for several seconds before crouching down beside her.

"I'm so sorry... I'm so sorry." It sounded like a mantra.

"No... it's... okay," she breathed. "I should... have... looked..."

Brushing her filthy hair from her face, he stared into her eyes. "I should have said something about it too."

"You came back for me. That's all that matters."

They shared a brief moment of relief before Cannon's eyes widened in alarm.

"We've got to wash you off. Now. Otherwise, you'll become encased in dried mud."

Fear ripped through Ryver once more. She may have been out of the sinkhole, but it was not done with her. If she didn't wash off the muck that slicked her body, she would slowly surrender to its merciless embrace once more. Who needed a jungle full of boa constrictors when you had ground that could squeeze you to death?

"Over here, I hear the sound of water," Cannon said, his eyes searching with quick, darting movements.

Sure enough, a small stream was nearby. It wove and tucked a small plume of water through the underbrush. Finding a bend in it where the water slowed and was deeper, Cannon helped Ryver douse herself.

Even in the thick of darkness, she could see the water darken as the sludge was freed from her clothes, returning to the earth through the ribbons of water.

They worked rapidly, scooping water and scrubbing at her clothing until most of the sludge had been removed. Slowly, the clasping grip of the gritty mud loosened its hold on her. She breathed deeper with every splash.

After several minutes, they stopped. Most of the mud was gone, but now they were faced with another problem.

Ryver was freezing. The water, though life-saving in one instance, now posed another threat. Cannon frantically searched in his bag for more clothing but came up empty.

"We n-n-n-eed to k-k-keep moving," Ryver chattered through her teeth. "We've been stopped for too long."

Flicking up his head from his search within the bag, Cannon growled in exasperation. "Can you walk?"

"I d-d-don't have a ch-ch-choice. We h-h-have to go," Ryver replied. All told, she would rather freeze than suffer being buried alive. Freezing seemed more humane, somehow.

"Wait just a second," he said and pulled her into a tight hug. Suddenly warmth surrounded her and the ice cold clothing started drying. She gasped but allowed herself to be warmed in his hug and then it stopped. Her clothes were still damp but no longer freezing and she was warm.

"You have a serious gift," she said. "To be able to warm people like that. Being a dragon shifter is amazing."

"I couldn't dry you more. I worried the heat would've gotten to be too much and I might burn you. So this is the best I could do. I wish I could dry you more."

She yanked his head down and kissed him. "Your best is great."

There was no denying the love growing for him in her heart. This man was doing everything in his power to not only protect her, but care for her. He treated her like she was already his and it made it harder for her to not want to be. His protective nature and loving, caring ways were hard to fight off. And though she'd never been in love before, there was no doubt in her mind she was now. With a big bad dragon shifter that treated her better than any man ever had.

"We have to keep going," he said, hugging her tight once more.

She hugged him back and basked in the love she wasn't fighting any longer. "Let's go, my love."

They set off once more. The night was only halfway complete, and they had to use its cover of darkness to gather as much distance as they could as rapidly as they could.

Cannon stayed closer to Ryver as they walked. She sensed he was angry at himself for letting her slip into the sinkhole. She could not blame him, though. She had to be more careful. She could not rely on him to save her every time.

Now that she'd been warmed, it was as if her body remembered how tired she was. She somehow moved forward, like a child's automaton.

She lost track of how long they walked or how far. It was comforting to know that every step took them farther from danger. She placed her solace in that. For that, along with Cannon's companionship, was all that was left to her.

Soon, the dawn arrived, pushing its way into the night sky. Ryver's spirits lifted a little at the sight.

"We'll make camp here," Cannon announced, choosing a patch of grass and branches surrounded by several large stones. It was concealed from their main path and afforded them a slight windbreak.

"Strip," he said.

Ryver looked at him, confused.

"We need to warm you up more," he explained after seeing her reaction. "Those damp clothes for all those hours were not good for you."

She pulled on her clothes but exhaustion made it hard.

"Allow me," he said, coming over to her.

Once again, she was sheepish that he needed to help her. But she decided she no longer cared. He was here to help her. And right now, she was willing to take all the help she could get.

TWENTY

CANNON

His deft fingers helped her with her clothes. Her body shivered with cold and exhaustion, but her face betrayed no discomfort. He didn't think he could think more highly of her than he already did, but his admiration for her grew.

And yet he had a sense of powerlessness as well. Though he had established a sleeping area by draping a tarp over some rocks that nestled together at the apex of the clearing where they made camp, he could not provide much more in terms of comfort.

A fire was out of the question. Though its warmth would be welcome, the light and smoke it would throw off would only bring any militia groups right to them. They might as well send up a flare.

They were nothing if not persistent, these guerrillas. Ryver and Cannon had thwarted them so far and against so many odds. He'd be damned if he got sloppy now.

Peeling off her sweatshirt, heavy with damp, Cannon took stock of her injuries. The side wound was healing nicely despite the insanity of the past couple of days. Various bruises and small cuts littered her creamy skin and, at the sight of each one, Cannon' sadness and an anger threatened to cloud his vision.

His shoulder blades ached. He knew why. Underneath those very human bones, his wings lay dormant until the bug in his neck was removed.

Oh, how he wished he could simply shift into his dragon form, gather her close, and fly out of danger completely. If he was unsuccessful, he could blame the general and their need to keep control over him.

Once again, the knowledge that the warden was Ryver's mom came to mind. At some point, he'd have to tell her– that the general was her mother. But how and would she even believe him?

Her sweatshirt was removed, and he helped

her with her pants, socks, and shoes. Her skin was cold to the touch, and she shivered. But not one word of complaint came from her lips.

Seeing her like this made him sick. The thought of losing her made him weak. When he'd found her in quicksand up to her chin, panic nearly paralyzed him. He was overconfident in his ability to keep her safe that he let the most innocuous of things almost take her life.

Knowing he could really lose her, that her humanity made her fragile, he realized how miserable his life would be without her in it. He would rather return to the prison than live with her gone. He had to admit his feelings were genuine, not just something to occupy the time.

No question. She was his mate. He understood this to the marrow of his bones.

Not in such a long time had he had any real reason to fight to remain alive. And now that he had that meaning, it was almost taken away from him. This was a new fight for him, a new perseverance to continue. God, he loved her. He loved this tiny human and wanted to protect her more than anything in the world.

With each piece of clothing he removed, he debated what he should do with it. Logic would dictate that he hang them over the surrounding rocks to dry. But that would be visible. The clothes, though dirty, were grayish-white – a dead giveaway in the velvety blackness of the night.

No, he could not simply hang them to dry. The next best solution was to drape them around the entrance to their makeshift tent. It wouldn't be perfect, but it would perhaps dry them slightly.

Ryver stood, shivering and silent, as Cannon went about hanging her clothes as best he could. Her breath was ragged. Cannon moved with purpose and speed, and when the clothes were arranged, he turned back to Ryver.

What he saw next frightened him more than anything else so far. Ryver's face and lips were turning blue. He knew instantly that her body was starting to shut down, and if he didn't heat her up immediately, he'd lose her.

If he wasn't about to lose her to terrorists, he wasn't about to lose her to the cold. Fuck that.

He couldn't light a fire. But he had body heat to spare.

"Ryver, how are you doing?"

He needed to hear her voice if only to confirm that she was still with him.

"C-c-old" was all she said.

Then, as if in slow motion, she folded slowly to the ground. Her shivering was sapping her strength, and she could no longer stand. Her body was on a slippery slope to hypothermia. She was losing heat faster than she could make it, and the body was starting to prioritize the vital organs.

And it was losing that battle.

Cannon stripped himself bare, tossing his clothes into their tent to make a bed.

"Come here, baby, come here," he whispered soothingly as he gathered her up and placed her within the tent.

Spooning her, he wrapped his own body around her, trying to cover every square inch of her with his own flesh. As he did so, he rubbed her back up and down, up and down, allowing the heat of his dragon to slowly seep from him into her and warm her up.

"All right now, all right. Let's get to know each other better, shall we? We've barely been able to have a real conversation, with all this escaping and all," he said, trying like hell to keep the fear out of his voice.

"N-n-no, we h-h-haven't," she whispered, the hint of a laugh in her reply.

"All right then. Well, let's do that now. No time

like the present," he said. His hands furiously worked up and down her back. Small patches of warmth bloomed there, and a small flame of encouragement grew inside him.

"O-k-k-k-kay."

Now wasn't the time to ask about her dead mother, though he so badly wanted to hear more about his mate's life. "What's your favorite color?"

"Re-r-r-ed," came the reply.

"Excellent choice. Mine as well." He moved to another section of her back and began moving his legs against hers to create even more heat and touching her and passing more of the dragon warmth to her.

"Any hobbies?"

A small giggle escaped from her between shivers. "B-books," she answered.

"Ah, that's where we differ. Not one for books. But I respect them," he replied.

A little laugh. Another good sign. More heat radiated underneath his hands and legs from him to her. Her temperature was heading in the right direction.

"Cats or dogs?" He realized everything was absurd right now, but he had to keep her awake – at least until her body righted itself.

"D-dogs" came the answer. The ebbed slowly. The muscles in her back begin to slacken as he infused them with heat.

"That's my girl. Cats and dragons have an odd history. Dogs love us no matter what."

"Allergic," she replied.

"Ah, well, that will do it too. But for me? Can't trust a cat."

Another chuckle. This time, her sigh traveled between them. The shivering slowed even more. Her breath became more stable. Only a few more minutes, and then she would be out of danger.

"Beatles or Rolling Stones?"

"That's easy. Be-Beatles."

"Huh. You surprise me. Thought you'd be a Stones gal."

"You?"

"Stones, baby. All the way."

She sighed once more, and he noticed, with a flare of relief, that her body had completely stopped shivering. Her skin was warm, and her breathing was back to normal underneath him and around him.

"Gimme shelter," she whispered. He laughed, and a moment later, he noticed she was asleep. He was only too happy to let her do so. Her body had been through so much.

Minutes passed. He continued to cover her body with his, occasionally running his hands up and down her back to ensure the heat was still there.

Satisfied that she was now completely warm, he realized that he, too, was exhausted. But he could not let himself fall into a deep slumber. That would be too dangerous.

Closing his eyes, he forced himself to stay just one layer below being fully conscious. He was aware of the wind, the distant hum of flowing water, the occasional night predator making a kill. But most of all, he was aware of the steady breathing of Ryver beneath him.

Just hearing that steady rhythm calmed him and gave him hope they would get out of this country in one piece.

A few hours passed, and his ears picked up no sounds of anyone coming near. He knew they had to move on soon but wanted to eke out each and every minute of respite they could.

Ryver's body then stretched. With a deep inhalation, she arched her body into his. Cannon's eyes fluttered open, and he saw that dawn's light was nudging its way into their makeshift tent.

To his vast relief, he also saw that Ryver's body was pink and healthy, flushed with warm, life-giving blood. His mate was perfect once again.

She turned her body to face him, their warmth scattering and reconnecting. Her eyes looked deep into his, the irises huge in the low light of a new day.

"Morning," she whispered.

"Morning."

"Thank you."

"For what?"

Gently, she kissed him, their lips only barely touching.

"For saving my life."

"Anytime."

They stayed like that for several seconds before she spoke once more. "Beatles Forever."

He laughed in the early morning light.

TWENTY-ONE

RYVER

Ryver was finally warm, and she was beyond thankful that Cannon was there for her. She could have frozen to death if he hadn't been there to help her. The temperature drop and her damp clothes had been a recipe for disaster. She was sure she'd have a panic attack worrying about what would happen to her. But Cannon had a way of calming her, of easing her pain, that no one in her distant memory was ever capable of.

She stared deeply into his eyes and ran her hands over his face and chest. She could see the relief on his face that she was fine. He smiled broadly. "Are you okay?"

She was beyond okay. She knew she had fallen

head over heels for this man, in this situation out of all conditions. She wanted to escape with him right now, to fly off into the distance with him and thrive on some mountain where no one would see them. It seemed absurd, but it was the sweetest of daydreams at that moment.

His body was warm too, which had warmed her all over. It also warmed her loins, and she wanted him so badly.

"Cannon, I want you."

Cannon frowned but was also aroused. She could see his erection rising through the blanket that covered them. She reached down and touched his hardness. He flinched.

"Ryver, what are you doing?"

"I think you know what I'm doing. Just want to celebrate life." Ryver leaned in close and kissed him. Her eyes closed as his tongue move around her mouth. She moaned and moved her hand up and down his shaft.

He grunted against her touch. He pulled away from her kiss, smiling. "You're spectacular, Ryver."

"I want to have all of you. You do so much to take care of me, and I want to show you how much I appreciate you." Ryver's voice was low and seductive, and it seemed to be working.

She touched his chest, then began pushing him backward. "Lie back," she ordered.

Cannon raised his eyebrows but followed suit, slowly lying on his back. She continued to play with him, moving a single hand up and down his hardness. He groaned, loving her touch.

She loved making him feel good. She brought her second hand to his shaft, needing both fists to wrap around his thickness. His eyes rolled back into his head. "Good lord, Ryver, you're amazing."

Ryver smiled. This man was her rescuer, and being able to admit that meant something vulnerable inside her was finally coming to life. She was never able to disclose this kind of feeling to anyone, so having them now and being able to express them enthralled her.

"You're the amazing one. It's my turn to take care of you now." Ryver placed two fingers at the entrance of her hood and played with her clit. It was swollen and wet, so ready to take on his cock. Cannon watched her as she relished in the sensation of herself and moved her remaining hand up and down his hard dick.

She moaned against herself. Cannon reached out and touched her arms, his warmth encouraging her actions. She knew that she had become slick enough to take in his size, so she lifted her pelvis and held her wetness directly over his shaft.

Cannon stopped her, holding her by the arms. "Be careful, Ryver. I don't want you to hurt yourself."

Ryver appreciated his concern. She smiled down at him, reassuring him with her broad grin. "I'll be gentle, don't you worry."

She gripped his dick in one hand and settled herself onto him with the other. It was a slow and careful process, as he filled her like a balloon that was going to burst. But she knew she could take him; she had taken him in before. But it was never in this position.

She wanted to have control this time. She wanted to be the one giving him the pleasure. He was such a thoughtful lover, one she'd always craved, and now she could give that back to him.

Ryver had him inside her, and the sensation transcended pleasure. Her eyes widened as she took him in completely, putting her legs on either side of his torso. For a second, they were both silent and still. Then Ryver got a hold of herself and began minutely bouncing on top of him.

Cannon looked up at her with amazement. That was the look she wanted to see, and it was a look that made her feel even wetter. She lifted her pelvis slightly higher, guiding his penetrating cock deeper into her welcoming pussy.

"Oh, woman, what are you doing to me?" Cannon asked, eyes wide and blazing in the dark. She was riding him in the soft dirt with very little light around them to highlight the frame of their naked bodies. She moaned softly, completely leaning into the feeling of all-embracing carnal pleasure.

She imagined what it would be like to fuck him on a bed, in the shower, in the comfort of their own home. She could bellow and moan all she wanted. She could make him feel things with orgasms he'd never experienced before. She bit down on her lip with her eyes closed, lightly increasing her speed on top of him. She loved being in this position – she was a sexy goddess.

Cannon stroked her breasts. She gave in to his touch, moaning as he played with her nipples. It was overwhelming being with Cannon, but it was the only way she wanted to feel.

The memory of having multiple near-death experiences had evaporated entirely from her mind as she fucked Cannon in the middle of the jungle. Both of them were naked and hot, with sweat from grinding up against one another. His dick was jabbing at her G-spot, and she knew she would come soon, but she wanted to focus on his pleasure this time.

So she began grinding harder. It wasn't painful but more filling. Cannon grabbed her again. "Slow down, Ryver. You're going to hurt yourself."

She swatted his hands away, then grabbed them. She placed both of his hands back on her breasts and began moving them in a circular motion. "Please trust me, love. Let go."

Desire dazzled in Cannon's eyes. She watched him as he bucked against her while she rode him faster and faster. Her sounds were louder and more sporadic with every stroke of her insides. Her body was aflame, and she knew Cannon's was as well. She watched his body clench and unclench, push and then stop.

"Come on, my big bad dragon," Ryver almost shouted. "Give me everything."

Cannon growled, then grabbed her by the thighs. He lifted his hips and rocked himself upward, moving deeper into her tightness. Ryver yelped and gave a mischievous grin. She began riding him faster and harder, bouncing up and down like he was the most fun trampoline ride of her life.

And indeed, he was.

"Oh fuck, Ryver, I can't...hold...back..."

Cannon squeezed his eyes shut. Ryver loved the feel of his dick quivering inside her. He let himself go and came inside her. Hot. Hard. The sensation of beautiful wetness made her eyes roll back. She rode him softly and slowly as whispers of eruptive post-orgasmic movements took him over. She slowly pulled him out and lay next to him.

He continued to moan and breathe heavily. Ryver was smiling, then touched his lips with her fingers. "I could do that every day for the rest of my life."

Cannon turned to look at her. "I can't believe you did that without hurting yourself! I was so worried."

Ryver kissed him passionately; the look of fear melted off his face. Immediately he moved his fingers down to her sensitive clit. She jumped at his touch. "Now it's your turn."

Ryver lay back and let Cannon's fiery fingers take her over. It took her no longer than twenty seconds to fly over the edge, shaking her body against him and biting his neck as her orgasm moved through her like a steady stream. They fell back into each other's arms in the darkness, reveling in post-coital delight.

"I don't think I'll ever be cold again," Ryver whispered.

Cannon laughed, then kissed her cheek. "You definitely will never be as long as I'm around."

TWENTY-TWO

CANNON

The light of the moon woke Cannon from his slumber. The sight in itself was pleasant, but he knew it had previously exposed their position. It allowed them to see their way better, though, which avoided more issues in itself. He thought about the pros and cons as he shook Ryver awake.

He was feeling more tired than he ever had in his life. Exhaustion wasn't anything new for the shifter, but they were more likely to bounce back faster than humans. His adrenaline had been moving for the past few days, fight and then fucking, walking in the night and sleeping in the day. He was thankful he had Ryver with him, but he could also use a good night's rest.

He hoped that they could both get what they needed soon.

He hated waking her, and she looked so calm. But he knew that they had to get going. He wanted to get out of that place soon and begin their lives together.

Ryver sat up, rubbing her eyes. "It's time to go already?"

Cannon knelt and pushed her hair out of her face. She was beautiful. Under the moonlight, her eyes swam. He kissed her and smiled. "Looks like it. We shouldn't be far now. My animal's sense of direction brought us back to our original track after detouring south at the last village."

She stretched, reaching her tiny frame toward the sky. Cannon couldn't help but hug her and lift her slowly. Ryver yelled sarcastically, and he kissed her during her shout. She kissed him back. Cannon was in a daydream.

He put her down, and she smiled at him. He wished they weren't in this situation, but he had to be positive.

He took out their remaining food supply, and she gulped it down. He had filtered some water into a bottle, so they could also hydrate. Ryver finished their drink, then stood next to Cannon. She looked at him with great interest.

"What?" he asked, smiling.

"I'm just learning so much about shifters. It's interesting because you look so human, but you have so many features that I don't."

"It's all about enhancement. Other than the actual shifting part, we are only humans with enhanced abilities."

"And yours is mostly strength?"

Cannon nodded. He loved how interested she was in his life. "Strength, smell, intuition, everything is heightened. That's why it was so strange being in that prison. It was like a shackle for your mind."

Ryver reached up and touched his face. "You'll never be back there again, I promise."

Could she make that promise to him? Cannon didn't want to think about it. Instead, he kissed her lightly, then pointed toward the path.

"Let's stay slightly off the path because of the moon, but we can still use it for light."

Ryver nodded, her playful face fading to a serious expression. They went in the direction and followed between seemingly endless rows of trees.

They silhouetted against the moon, and Cannon was calm for about an hour as they walked. He and Ryver intermittently held hands like they were on a romantic date.

"So, is this what we're going to be doing when we get back?"

They held hands as Ryver inquired. Cannon could feel his face going red for the first time in his life.

"What, walking with very little clothing in the moonlight?"

Ryver laughed. "Well, maybe something a little more comfortable than that."

Cannon squeezed her hand as he spoke. "It's been a while since I've been on a date, but let me think – do you prefer wine or beer?"

"Either or, but wine for this situation."

"Okay," Cannon continued. "Let's get a bottle of wine and head out into the park. Maybe it's nighttime, but not this late. The moon will be high in the sky, and it'll be warm out. I'll bring a blanket and lay it out for us."

Ryver was nodding and smiling as he continued.

"I'll lay it out, and we will lie together, maybe

bring a telescope to look at the stars. It will be a clear night, of course."

"Will we make love?"

Cannon scoffs. "Of course, we will."

Ryver kissed his arm as they walked. "I want to know what it's like to fly with you. That must be something."

Cannon's heart skipped a beat. He never had anyone involved with him who wanted to see his dragon form or even be near it. Yet, her interest made him feel like he loved her even more.

"We can do that. It can be striking at first to fly, but over time you'll get used to it, and you'll love it."

Ryver squeezed his hand. "I know I will."

Suddenly, the wooded area stopped. Cannon also stopped with Ryver, noticing the open plain before them. His calm erupted into fear, knowing this would be a good place for an ambush on unexpecting travelers.

Cannon sighed out loud and stared out into the distance. There were a few shrubs and bushes, but it wasn't enough for them to hide. He also noticed a ravine in the space that wasn't concealed by the umbrella of trees. He was worried and tried not to show it.

Ryver pulled at his hand. "What are you thinking?"

Cannon looked down at her. She stared inquisitively, ready for action.

"I'm worried about how open this place is, but I see no way we can go around."

Ryver nodded. She looked determined but aided in easing Cannon's anxiety. "We'll just push through. You said we weren't that far, right?"

Cannon nodded.

"So let's go then." Ryver began walking forward hastily.

Cannon was still nervous, but he followed suit, taking each step ahead carefully. They were able to move through the field quickly. Cannon watched the tops of the trees while Ryver moved forward, looking for any threats. He loved the team they were becoming.

Soon enough, they reached the ravine. Under the light of the moon, it looked long and slightly treacherous. Cannon reminded Ryver that they needed to be extra careful.

"I don't think it's profound, but let's just be cautious – there could be fallen branches or anything moving around in here."

Ryver nodded. She was holding the backpack now and was directly behind him. They would move slower, but it was better that way to avoid injuring themselves.

Cannon tested the water. It was shallow, so he knew they could easily walk through it. When he stepped forward, something metallic pressed against his face.

"Don't move."

A man to the side of him held a gun, pressing it against his face. He wasn't wearing a mask like the others, but a bandana over his mouth. His clothes looked and smelled dirty. These weren't part of the militias or the terrorist chasing them earlier – they were random thieves looking to rob them.

Cannon did as he was told and tried to sense where Ryver was behind him. He could hear her screaming from beneath gloved hands. Another man must have taken her from behind and was covering her mouth.

"Don't hurt us," Cannon whispered. He had one foot in the ravine and the other on the ground. The man pushed the gun farther into his forehead. "Shut the fuck up, and we'll find out."

Cannon did as he was told. He had dealt with

many people like this, but no one was more dangerous than the desperate. He could sense their hunger, frustration, and willingness to do anything they could to get what they wanted from them. He could shift into his dragon form and fight them off, but he didn't know how many there were, nor what kind of weapons they had in their possession.

"Can you let my friend go?" Cannon whispered.

"What did I just fucking say?" The man with the gun brought it down hard on the top of Cannon's forehead. Cannon was a strong man, but the strike still hurt. He wavered slightly, maybe a bit exaggeratedly, to make them think he wasn't a force to be reckoned with. Make them feel they had the power, and then they would let their guard down.

"Turn the fuck around." The gunmen forced Cannon to turn toward Ryver. She was held with a knife to her throat and a man covering her mouth. The man also reeked of desperation and callousness.

"It's okay. We're going to be fine." To ease her fear, Cannon tried to bore his look deep into her eyes, even telepathically. But the men holding them weren't going to have anything of it. So instead, the man with the knife pressed harder into her neck as the gunman ordered them to their knees.

"Get down on the ground, and don't make a sound – I fucking mean it this time."

TWENTY-THREE

RYVER

Ryver had been watching Cannon place his foot into the water to test it when someone grabbed her from behind. One hand went around her mouth while the other pressed something sharp against her neck. To say that she was surprised was an understatement – she was immediately angry that she hadn't heard them coming.

A man then stood next to Cannon with a gun to his head. Her heart was pounding, absolutely terrified that something was going to happen to him. Finally, Cannon said something to the man, and the man struck him. Cannon wavered slightly, and Ryver screamed. She didn't know what else she could do at that moment.

She imagined taking the knife from the man and stabbing him. She had never really been violent, but she became vicious at that moment.

The man with the gun ordered Cannon to turn to face her. When he did, she saw Cannon's eyes. They were calm but also scared. She tried to tell him she would be okay with her look. But, instead, she saw him mouth the same thing to her.

"Now, get on your knees." The man with the gun ordered them. They did as they were told. Ryver's mind was racing. Where the fuck did they come from? They must have been waiting for some time behind the rocks because neither had seen them coming at all.

The man holding her still had a knife on her neck. The man with the gun seemed to be the leader, so he ordered them to hand over all of their things. "We don't have much," Cannon replied.

"I'll slice her up, I swear!" the man holding Ryver said, squeezing her tighter on her throat. She was scared. She wished she had shifting abilities because then she could shift and be the one to save Cannon. But then again, it could be too late since the man had a gun.

"Quiet!" the gunmen shouted at his friend.

The friend stayed quiet and let the leader take hold of the situation.

"Hand it all over, fucker." Cannon lifted his backpack off himself, then suddenly raised it as high as he could. It was still slightly heavy with the food they had left, so it smacked the gunmen on the chin swiftly. He leaped onto him and punched the gun out of his hands. It bounced into the water.

This made Ryver lunge forward, which caused the man who was holding her to lose his balance. He fell forward onto her back, and then she rolled and switched onto her back. She grabbed the hand that held the knife, then smacked it against the ground. The man screamed and eventually dropped the blade. The man stood, trying to reach for the knife, when she kicked him in the knee. She heard the snap as it bent in the opposite direction than it should be. She winced at the sound and at her ability to hurt someone. The man fell to the ground, screaming and holding his leg.

Cannon had the other man, half his body in the ravine, by the throat. He was holding him down, pressing him into the water. Ryver noticed he had his finger in his face and was screaming questions at him.

"Who do you work for! What the fuck do you want from us?"

Ryver knew that the man whose knee she kicked was no longer going to do any harm. She picked up the knife and shoved it into her pocket. She made her way over to him and grabbed him by the shoulders. He stopped choking the man immediately.

"I don't think they work for anyone."

Cannon held the man by the throat. The man recoiled, his face soaking. "I know that. But you never know, there are allegiances everywhere."

"I know." Ryver rubbed his back. She didn't want to seem condescending to him, but these were probably people who were down on their luck. She was filled with disgust that she had ruined that man's leg, probably for life.

Cannon stood, lifting the man with him. He held him for a moment, then threw him down. "Now, give us all *you* have." The gunmen scurried toward his injured friend – their bandanas had fallen, so now they could see that they were just kids. Kids looking to make an extra buck or two.

But Ryver could see how angry Cannon was. The fact that he was mad on her behalf was charming but frightening, considering that he could have easily ripped that boy's head off.

The men emptied their pockets, tossing other extra knives, some food, and a few coins. Cannon snapped his fingers at them. "Now strip."

The men looked at each other, bewildered.

Cannon bellowed at them. It was deafening. "What did I just say? That's what you were going to do to us, right?"

The men undressed as quickly as they could. Ryver stood next to Cannon as she watched him breathing, rage coating his insides. Finally, the men were completely naked, and Cannon ordered them to toss their clothes to them.

Cannon then pointed in the opposite direction. "Now go home. Don't do this shit anymore."

The men looked at Ryver for sympathy, but another roar cut it off from Cannon. "*Go*!"

They fled, their naked skin glowing under the moonlight. Cannon gathered their clothes and placed them on a rock, so if the boys returned, they could have them back, but he threw the weapons into the distance.

"You know, you didn't have to strip them. Who knows how far away they might live?" Ryver said.

Cannon was crouching when she said this. His

response wasn't directly to her but to the clothes beneath him. "They were about to do the same thing to us, Ryver. I'm sure they wouldn't have felt bad about it."

Ryver was slightly stunned to hear this coming out of this man's mouth. Sure, he was strong, but also so caring and gentle with her. Maybe this was the part of him who succeeded as a mercenary. Or the part that landed him in a shifter prison. He was a convicted felon.

Ryver sighed. "They looked so young."

"They were young. Why do you think I was relentless on them?" Cannon stood, towering over her. She looked up at him as the moon outlined his angry face. "They'll always remember this, and when they do, they'll be afraid to try it again. Then, hopefully, it'll scare them enough to stop."

Ryver thought about it. It made sense, but the menace she saw in his expression when he held the boy in the ravine scared her. She pressed lightly, trusting that he would hear her.

"I think maybe you went a little too far. They were kids."

Cannon's face was getting red with anger. It wasn't a sight Ryver wanted to see, but she also needed to be honest with him. He bore his look down at her. She didn't back down in the slightest.

"Kids can kill people too, Ryver. This isn't a situation where you're going to talk them down. They were ready to kill us. The man had a knife to your throat. The other had a gun on me. This could have been over... completely over."

Ryver nodded. "I know that, but it isn't."

"Not because they changed their minds," he said, his eyes blazing.

"Okay, fine. I see where you're coming from. You did the right thing."

Cannon outreached his hand. "I know I did. Now give me the knife."

She frowned. "What?"

"You won't be needing it if you aren't going to be violent."

It was her turn to roll her eyes. "I think we can use it when it is necessary."

Cannon decided not to respond to this. Instead, he simply nodded and turned toward the ravine. Ryver agreed that she would let it go for the time being but would keep it in mind to talk about later.

"Let's get going. Those bastards slowed us down enough."

They resumed their original positions with Cannon in front, stepping into the ravine to test the waters. "Come," he said to Ryver.

She stepped into the water and was enveloped by a rush of wind. It was sharp and foreboding.

Once again, she wondered if this side of Cannon was created by being a merc or if the prison had done this to him. A mild fury erupted in her thinking about that place. If it was the last thing she did, she was going to have every shifter released and maybe even force a public apology by the government.

She said, "Tell me more about the prison. Who was in charge of the place?"

TWENTY-FOUR

CANNON

He was bothered by what Ryver had said about his treatment of the kids who had tried to rob them. They had been struggling for survival, and then they had to deal with local idiots? Plus, her life was threatened, and he had grown to have intense feelings of love for her. Did she think it was unreasonable to inquire forcefully about who sent them?

It had hurt him, and part of that was also kind of amazing. The fact that he could even feel hurt by someone was an entirely new development within itself. He had cut off emotions to anyone who wasn't worth it. But maybe feeling these things was worth it.

He wondered about those two young boys. He

wanted to feel bad for them, but he didn't. Behaviors had consequences, and he gave them theirs on a silver platter.

"Tell me more about the prison. Who was in charge of the place?" Ryver said.

Cannon shook his head. He was staring ahead, doing everything he could to move them along. The marshy ground told him they were getting closer to their rendezvous point. Once they reached the lake bordering the neighboring country, he'd breathe easy, but right now, his heart was pumping hard in his chest, so hard, it was coming up his throat.

How could he possibly tell her that her mother was a ruthless, uncaring human who had treated his kind like wild animals? He thought that about the woman, but he didn't know the shoes she walked in. When he was a child, no one thought he'd grow up and be a hired killer before trying to make himself a better person. He didn't know her whole story, so it wasn't his place to make Ryver hate someone he had limited experience with. He'd have to have faith it would all work out.

Instead of answering, he asked his own question. "First, tell me why hasn't the military appealed to you at all? Since your father made it his career."

Ryver stared ahead, eyes not focused on anything. "It's the moral of everything. I hated all of it. It was never about helping. My father tried to appeal to me by telling me I could help people, but I saw the truth of it."

Cannon replied into her ear. "That makes sense. So helping is important to you?"

She shrugged. "Yeah. Being a doctor seemed like something that would contribute to the world rather than destroy it."

Cannon admired her honesty. She knew that he was ex-military and had spent most of his life involved in some way, shape, or form. But she came from a place of morality, and he loved and admired that about her.

"Now, answer my question," she said.

Well, shit. He'd hoped she'd forget about it. "The prison was a standard prison."

"I call bullshit, Cannon. Don't try to sugarcoat it for me. I'm a big girl. How was the treatment? Did you get to go outside? How was the food? Answer me that?"

He gritted his teeth. He didn't want her to worry about him. "I'd had better..."

"Cannon," she warned.

He sighed. "The food was a step above slop for a pig."

When she didn't say anything, he glanced back at her. Rage seethed from her in waves. His heart filled with emotion. No one had ever cared how he was treated, what he suffered through. Not only did this woman care for him but all of his kind.

"You know," he said, "it's okay to show emotions sometimes. You don't always have to keep them bottled inside." Look who was calling the kettle black. But if he could help her feel better, he'd risk his man card.

For a moment, Ryver was silent. Then she sighed. "You're right. I'm not very good at admitting when I'm emotional. But you always can tell when I am. I want you to know..." Her voice faded out, but Cannon waited. She spoke up soon enough. "I want you to know everything. I've never wanted that from anyone before."

Cannon stopped and turned to her as she stepped up to him and leaned into him. She was so warm, and he would love just to stay there and revel in her touch. But he had to keep going. He pushed against the terrain.

He took her hand and stepped up on the edge

of the rock, looking out onto the mysterious tapestry. They both breathed in and took in the moment as keenly as they could. The bright moon beamed onto the landscape, making the dew on leaves sparkle like diamonds.

It amazed him how something so serene could be so deadly. What more would they encounter before reaching safety? He would do whatever it took to get this incredible woman home.

TWENTY-FIVE

CANNON

To his surprise, the ravine ahead of them was filled in with dirt, tree trunks, and debris. It looked like a dam had busted, and a flash flood had deposited all its contents here.

Cannon knew it would be a challenging time getting through all that fucking mess. They had to be careful just in case they came into contact with further sinkholes.

Cannon stepped forward, remembering there was a slight drop below them. He touched it with one foot, then placed another foot down. It was soft beneath him, so he began guiding Ryver down with him. She stepped carefully, making sure she planted her feet in the same spot where he stepped. Finally, he decided they couldn't move along the original path he had intended.

"Let's go along this way." Cannon pointed along the right side of the ravine. He couldn't recall any sinkholes, so he grabbed a long piece of nearby branch that was drooping down. "I'm going to use this to check out the space in front of us. Make sure you move with my steps. I don't want us to fall into anything."

Ryver nodded. He could see how tired she was. Even though they just talked about how to admit her fear, he knew it would take some time before she could open up completely. It had been a stormy night, and even he wanted to get some shut-eye.

"No problem," she said. "We should head out."

Cannon smiled, then began stepping ever so cautiously. He couldn't see the end of the ravine but decided that he didn't want to worry about that just yet. One step at a time.

They moved at a snail's pace. Cannon knew this would cause them to lose precious time, but he hadn't considered random thieves attempting to steal their supplies in the night.

"So about a week ago, you told your guy on the

walkie-talkie we were doing plan B. What's in Uganda?" she asked.

"The Infectious Disease Institute is there."

"I knew that!" she gasped. "They do a lot for the healthcare system in Africa. Are we going there?"

"No, thankfully. An A.L.F.A agent on assignment there will be meeting us at the lake on the western border."

"I heard you say A.L.F.A, but didn't understand. What's A.L.F.A?" she asked.

"Yeah. The Alpha League of Agents. They are the legal side of shifter mercenaries."

"Legal, as in they work for the government?"

"A long time ago, their group made a deal to keep their freedom by 'volunteering' four of their male shifters to work as undercover agents globally."

"Are they CIA shifters, basically?"

He shrugged. "Similar, but they deal with some weird shit."

She smiled. "Coming from a shifter, what is your definition of 'weird shit'?"

"Well, right. But we're talking demons, magic, and that kind of thing. At least I deal with things I can touch and smell. And understand."

"Is our contact a dragon too?"

"I'm not sure what he is. Feline, I believe."

Ryver was excited to talk with this agent. Maybe he could help her free the other shifters and change their world for the better.

About a half hour through the ravine, Cannon thought they had successfully made it past that portion of their journey. The mud in front of them was thinning but could still conceal any potential dangers. Ryver pulled against his hand. Cannon noticed that the moon was falling and the sun's peak was starting to show its glow over the horizon.

They stopped near a tall drift of wood and small boulders. Ryver almost ran directly into him, not realizing he had stopped. "Oh shit, I'm sorry."

Cannon touched her arms. She had been in autopilot mode as they walked, a common symptom of extreme fatigue. Nevertheless, he didn't think she was weak. After all, she was human and probably experiencing some trauma from everything she had been through.

"All good. I think we should stop right now and try to get some rest."

Ryver looked out ahead of them. The area was not wooded but blanketed with a thin dusting of sand. "Aren't we too exposed out here? I could keep going for a bit. Don't worry about me."

Cannon pointed at the mound of broken trees. "They aren't likely to see us if I use that as camouflage on the tent."

Ryver nodded. "That makes sense."

Cannon knew that Ryver was giving into exhaustion even if she didn't. He had been there before many times in prison. The implant drained him of his strength, of all of his power, and it was easy to fall into extreme bodily fatigue. That was probably what she was feeling right then and there.

Cannon removed the tent from his pack as Ryver sat on the sand. She put her face in her hands. Cannon could feel his heart swelling. "I know you don't like it when I ask you this all the time but are you really okay?"

Ryver laughed into her hands. "I mean, as okay as someone can be when they're being chased all over a country they don't know much about while dealing with the elements that are horrible."

Cannon was putting the tent together as he listened. Ryver had mastered the art of sarcasm, something not every person could understand. It could be hurtful to the average person, but it was her defense mechanism. It was a filter, a way in which she could say what she meant without actually saying it.

"I'm sorry, Ryver."

She looked up at him from the ground. Her blue eyes swirled with tears. "You don't have to keep saying that. I know you are, and this isn't your fault. I'm just an emotional mess right now."

Cannon had finished putting the tent together, then tossed some sand around it so it could blend it from above. He shook off the blanket and placed it inside. He held it open for Ryver to crawl inside. She did without a word.

He rubbed his hands up and down her back when they were both lying down. Finally, he whispered into her ear. "I'm only sorry that you're in this situation at all. It doesn't seem fair you are suffering for wanting to make the world a better place."

She nodded against his arm. "You're right, but that doesn't change anything."

They were too tired for such a serious conversation. He reached for his pack and took out a few protein bars and some jerky. "We should probably eat first before we get to sleep..."

In the middle of his sentence, Cannon heard the light snores coming from Ryver. His heart soared. There was nothing this woman could do wrong. He had never known any emotion like this before in his long, shifter life.

He tucked the food back into his pack and lay next to her. They would eat when she awoke. There was no point in waking her now. Rest was good for the mind and body. Cannon drifted off to sleep, breathing her sweet and calming scent.

TWENTY-SIX

RYVER

Ryver woke, not realizing that she had completely fallen asleep like a rock. Cannon was asleep behind her, soundly breathing. She stared at him for a moment, imagining a life outside this situation. She would love to continue this when multiple terrorist organizations weren't chasing them.

But would he want to do that? Was this just going to be some sexy affair that he forgot about and flew away to live on some mountain like he'd always wanted to? Would he just simply forget about her?

She wouldn't blame him if that was what he did. He had been in a shifter prison, and it could be likely that his main goal was to escape and be able to be his dragon-self at any point he wanted. Not that it was something Ryver would complain about.

Ryver decided to go back to sleep and let go of that thought. It would only give her more anxiety, and she was already having trouble with that while her life was in danger.

She awoke a few hours later to find Cannon eating quickly in the tent. He smiled at her as she sat up. "I hope I didn't wake you."

"No, I was already waking up. Do you think we should head off soon?"

Cannon nodded. "We're getting closer to the border. And, Ryver, I thought since the land is mostly clear of forest along the waterway, I could shift, and you could just ride me for a while."

Ryver grinned. "That's fine with me. But, you know, I'm open to all kinds of riding with you."

Cannon blinked, not realizing initially what Ryver was implying, but soon enough grinned with a naughty look in his eye. "Oh. Well, we can see about that later."

Ryver could feel her center warming for him. That was all it took, a few words and a look.

Ryver gathered up the tent into the pack and ensured it was secure. Cannon had given her a few protein bars to eat, but she only ate one. A part of her was nervous to see Cannon shift again while the other was excited. It wasn't every day you saw the man you loved turn into an animal. It somehow made him even more attractive to her.

"So to make this easier," Cannon said as he lifted his shirt off.

Ryver raised her eyebrows, trying not to be distracted by his rippling chest and back. "Yes?"

Cannon smiled, noticing her noticing him. "I don't have a lot of extra clothes left that aren't covered in grime, so I'm going to shift in the nude. How does that sound?"

Ryver nodded, holding the backpack out. "You know I'll never complain about seeing you naked."

Cannon blushed. "Well, that certainly helps me." He smiled at her and continued removing his clothing. The moon was waning, so it wasn't as bright as the night before. But it was still enough light to cast a luminescence onto his chiseled body, appearing in a natural spotlight.

"Okay, stand back. I won't hurt you, but the tail can get pretty long."

Ryver did as she was told. Cannon stood still and upright, then closed his eyes. The whole forest seemed to still be within that moment.

Ryver watched intently as colors flourished as they burst out of Cannon's skin in thick scales. His jaw grew larger, bones snapping to accommodate the growth of the lizard-like mouth. His eyes enlarged. Teeth sharpened into giant knives protruding from his lips. He had grown in height, with a thick scaled neck. Once he finished, he roared, eyes still squinted shut.

If Ryver didn't know him, she would probably be terrified. Instead, her heart was slamming in her chest, but she was excited to be a part of something so important to this man and his life.

Cannon opened his eyes. The bloodshot red glowed in the moonlight. He grinned, a thousand more teeth winking in the night. He growled and used his head to gesture to his back.

Ryver stepped forward, but she touched his scales before she climbed on top of him. They were thick and robust, like a lizard. Their shades reflected a rainbow in the moonlight. Cannon looked at her. Ryver looked back. She knew this was the person she loved. They wordlessly accepted one another before she lifted a leg and climbed up. She wrapped her arms around his neck before he launched forward into a gallop.

Ryver's gut leapt into her throat once they

glided across the ground. She trusted him, but her body had never experienced anything that was such an adrenaline rush. She clung to him as they maintained speed and an even flow.

When they came to a stop, Ryver had found her comfort zone, nestled into his neck and sensing his breathing. She found it soothing.

Cannon settled near a heavily wooded area. He lowered his neck so Ryver could climb down. When she did, he shifted back, standing away from her so his tail wouldn't whip her head. Ryver watched as he shrank, the scales absorbed into his skin, and his jaw shifted into its average human size.

He was naked again, so Ryver pulled out a blanket and wrapped it around him. She hugged him from his waist. "That was incredible, Cannon."

Cannon turned and embraced her while wearing the blanket. His skin was warm as if the transition had heated him. "I'm glad you were okay. I know it's a lot to deal with, but eventually, you get used to it." He kissed the top of her head. "I would never let you fall. Just wait till I get my wings back."

"What do you mean?" He had wings? How cool was that?

He grimaced and looked away. "A consequence of the implant by the general is that my wings won't shift. That's their way of making sure I don't disappear before the job was done."

Oh, now she was really pissed off. How could someone do that to another person? She would expose this military general-warden and everything about the shifter's plight to bring them into the world of human civil rights and luxuries. But first, she had to get off this damn continent.

Then she looked around, suddenly aware of the new surroundings. "So, where do we go from here? How much farther to the rendezvous point. We've been going for days."

Cannon shook his head. "I sense we're safe here, so you can relax. If my dragon's inner GPS is correct, this is the last stretch of trees before the lake. We can rest now before we move on."

Ryver agreed. She was feeling sweaty and heard the stream nearby once again. She pointed into the distance. "I'm going to rinse off a bit, okay? Won't be long."

Cannon winked, then continued building the tent.

When she was in the stream, she was completely naked. Although a part of her was paying attention to the sign of any of the terrorists, most of her mind had gone wild, on fire with desire.

Her thoughts went to Cannon and she became completely turned on. But she didn't want to experience that alone.

She picked up her clothes and made her way back to Cannon.

Cannon was just finished building the tent when he spotted Ryver, completely naked.

"Fuck, aren't you a sight!" he said, clearly taken aback but happy about what he was seeing.

"You like what you see?" She teased.

"Hell yes."

"Then come and get some, my big bad dragon."

TWENTY-SEVEN

CANNON

Cannon stared at Ryver's gracefully curved back, his pulse thundering through his ears. She peeked over her shoulder, silken mane swept to the side. The mix of shyness and desire in her gaze left him dry mouthed.

"Ryver." Her name caressed his tongue like a velvet gloved lover. "I—I want you so much. I don't want to hurt you."

"You won't, Cannon," she said, a smile tugging the corners of her sensual lips. "I trust you."

Cannon moved in on her, his hands caressing her shoulders. Ryver sighed, tilting her head back and letting her soft tresses cascade down his arm. He let his hands slide down the soft, pliant perfection of her skin, down to her waist, and over her flared hips.

He leaned in, his breath coming in hot pants, and kissed her on the neck. Ryver let out a soft sigh, leaning into him, eyes closed in a blissful repose. He kissed her neck again.

Cannon slid his hand around her body and caressed her breasts. He lifted her sweet soft roundness, taking the weight of the world into his hand quite literally. His finger and thumb teased her nipple, feeling it harden into arousal.

"Oh, yessss," she sighed. "I love it when you touch me."

He caressed her belly, hand sweeping down to the warm, wet folds of flesh between her legs. Cannon found her clit and gently stroked it with sensual circles of his fingertip.

She pressed herself into him, giving herself over. He turned her about to face him, pressing her back to the bark of the tree. Her smile made his heart thud harder in his chest. Love for his beautiful mate overflowed through him.

"My beauty. I want you more than I can say."

She gasped, biting her lower lip and looking at him with burning need in her eyes. He knew it only reflected his own gaze. Never had Cannon burned for a woman as much as he burned for Ryver.

He took her lips then, crushing his own over them. Something between a whimper and a moan escaped through her lips into his mouth. Cannon's tongue moved inside her mouth, probing and claiming its stake.

She lashed her own against it, amid a symphony of gasps, pants, and soft sighs. Their naked bodies pressed flush against each other, the only barrier remaining sweat and heat. Cannon kissed his way down her neck, moving inexorably toward her soft, pliant breast.

He popped her nipple inside his mouth and sucked. His tongue flicked over her hardening nub even as he moved his hands downward.

Cannon gently lifted her right leg and draped it over his shoulder as he released her nipple. She gasped as this move put his face right in her pussy.

"Oh, my," she moaned. "You're so good at this."

He greedily lapped her folds, running his tongue between her swollen lips before giving each of them a through lick. He moved to her inner lips, moving his tongue in slow circles. His nose pressed into her mound, and her whole pussy twitched.

The smell of her arousal filled his senses. Her

nails scraped at his scalp, her mouth open to let out pleasure-filled soft cries.

He wanted her to feel the utmost pleasure. Her pussy's slick wetness fueled his desire like the corona of a dying star. He pressed his face into her, moving his lips up to envelop her clit.

"Cannon," she cried, throwing her head back. A piercing cry split the air with every suck on her clit. Her nails dug into his scalp, her body thrashed against the tree, but Cannon didn't stop or slow down until his face was wet with her orgasm.

She arched over him, hair trailing down his bare shoulder as she shivered with the power of her climax. he gently held her in his arms, stroking her hair and adoring the way she came for him.

"That was amazing," she purred. "Again. You never disappoint."

"We've only just begun."

He kissed her, slowly pushing her into the tree. He caressed her well rounded ass and she thrust it against him as if in sudden relief. They gave themselves over to mutual desire.

He positioned himself behind her and ran his cock through the pink space between her swollen pussy lips. She moaned and groaned with every stroke over her slick flesh.

Then, he pushed the tip of his cock inside of her. He gasped as he leaned into his first thrust, filling her completely.

"Oh god," she moaned. "I love this. You're amazing."

He gritted his teeth and gave her a long, slow stroke. His body glided into her own, cock balls deep in her pussy. Her mouth flew open in a sharp cry.

"Oh yes," she moaned. "Oh Cannon, oh god..."

"You're so perfect," he gasped, blinking sweat out of his eyes.

He gripped her ass for leverage and slammed harder into her. She moaned in a high-pitched tone, slightly startled by the intensity of his penetration. But she continued to encourage him, moving rhythmically at his pace.

Desire blurred his mind. But she kept up with him, giving as good as she got.

His dick rubbed her deep. And she responded to it every time they collided. Her fingers curled into the branches she held onto for support.

"Oh please. Don't stop. Don't stop. I'm so close..."

As he slammed his cock into her, her pussy clenched and squeezed him hard, holding him hostage. Her body seized, then quivered. Her breath sputtered out of her, and she nearly collapsed onto the tree in front of her. Cannon held her up.

"Oh, oh fuck," she whispered. Cannon loved her pleasure. It was a sacred sound. He continued moving in and out until he came so hard he roared.

He shuddered, his cock deep inside her and her pussy muscles clenching around him. Finally, he moved on top of her, hovering over her torso.

He breathed heavily along with her breaths. For a long moment, it was only them and their breathing. In the darkness, their love had filled that corner of the world. They needn't say anything to one another because they were both feeling it profoundly.

Cannon pushed himself to stand and saw the hand marks he had left on her ass cheeks. He initially cringed, then had a flush of pride. He took Ryver by the shoulders, turned her around, and kissed her deeply. She moaned against him as she held onto his neck to maintain balance and pushed her mouth deeper into him.

Cannon never wanted that moment to end. He could kiss her forever, protect her forever, and keep her as his in infinite pleasure and comfort.

But he had to pull away eventually. When they did, they both remained breathless and smiling. "Holy shit," Cannon whispered to her.

"I'm glad we didn't go to the rendezvous right away." Her smiling was stunning, unlike anything he'd ever seen in his life. He wanted it to take him away from all of the pain he had ever had in his life. He reached out and stroked her with his fingers.

"Every second with you is a gift."

Ryver touched his hand, then kissed his fingers, one by one. "It was weird the way we met, but I am so thankful it was you who came to save me."

Cannon's heart filled with love. She shared the same feelings for him as he did for her.

"Let's rest for now and see where the day takes us."

TWENTY-EIGHT

CANNON

Cannon only let them doze in the tent for a little bit, as he knew it would take a certain amount of time to get to the rendezvous point. It had to be daylight, but he didn't want to be too late in the day. They were both still naked when they rose, so they left the tent and got dressed quickly. They both remained silent, and this slightly worried Cannon. He hoped that earlier hadn't been good-bye sex.

There was so much ahead for them to get out of this country, yet so much for them left in their relationship. He didn't want to lose her either way.

"Let's start walking, and we will probably make it just before daybreak."

Ryver nodded, placing the backpack on her,

not looking at him. Cannon held out his hand. "I can take that now."

Ryver shook her head. "I can deal with it."

Cannon's heart sunk. Had she returned to her closed-off self, even after sharing so much with one another, emotionally and physically? He continued, insistent.

"I'm hoping there isn't any resistance, but just in case, I want to have the pack near me so I can take out more ammo."

Ryver looked at him. Deep in her eyes was still fear of death. "Do you think that we can still be attacked out here?"

Cannon breathed deeply, then shrugged. "It isn't likely, but this place has surprised us a few times, so I'd rather be prepared."

Ryver took off the pack and handed it to him. Cannon held it before him for a minute, touching Ryver's hand.

"If anything happens, I know that you'll help us. There's an extra gun in here I can give you."

Ryver's eyes went wide. "I've never fired a gun before."

Cannon looked up at the sky. It was starting to look brighter, and he wanted to get going. "I don't think you'll need it, but I want you to know I have it."

Cannon checked the bag for ammo and reloaded his sidearm. Ryver stood with her hands in her pockets, looking concerned. When he finished, he placed his hand on her shoulder. "Are you okay?"

"As okay as I can be. But I just really want to get out of here."

Cannon kissed her. "I know. I promise we will get out of here."

She looked at him, her eyes filled with sadness, but he could not decipher what kind.

They walked along the wooded path. The only sounds were a few birds rising from sleep and a light gust of wind. Cannon was thankful they were almost at the end. But what would he do when he faced the general next?

They arrived at the country's border. An open field surrounding Lake Albert made Cannon a little nervous. He held Ryver by the hand when he removed his earpiece, finally working within that radio range. "A.L.F.A, come in. We're at the rendezvous point, over."

He heard static through his ear for a few moments, and then a familiar, sarcastic voice came over the line. Gus replied, "Well, long time no talk, brother. We've been ready to go for a week now."

Cannon rolled his eyes, which made Ryver giggle. "Put your asses in gear."

"Right you are, boss. Asses immediately in gear. We should be there in less than ten. Over and out."

Cannon removed the piece from his ear. "They'll be here soon. Let's hang tight until they do."

Ryver sighed. They were still holding hands just by the edge of the field near the trees. "You know what I've missed the most?"

Cannon listed intently. "What?"

"Ice cream. Ice cream and movies. That was my favorite thing as a kid. Sometimes my dad would rent multiple movies on the weekend. We'd get treats, ice cream, pizza, the usual. Then we'd watch a few movies in a row. I miss that."

Cannon touched the side of her face. He wanted to give her that, more than anything. But he also wanted to be with her when she did that.

"We'll get you back to your ice cream, babe. What's your favorite flavor?"

"Well, I'm an adult, so I don't have a favorite flav..."

They heard people speaking loudly behind them. Cannon grabbed Ryver by the arm, and they took cover behind a fallen log nearby. Cannon immediately removed the gun from his pack and handed it to her.

"I told you I don't know how to use this," Ryver whispered, irritated and frightened.

Cannon loaded the handgun, cocked it, and ensured that everything was in the right place. He put it in her hand. It looked heavy sitting there. "You don't have to learn everything right now. All you have to do is point and shoot. The trigger is here. It might kick back the first time and startle you, but after that, you'll get the hang of it. Just don't shoot me, and we'll be fine."

Ryver pursued her lips. Within that moment, he wanted to tell her what he was feeling. That he was in love with her, that he wanted to spend the rest of his life with her. He wanted to spend every weekend with her, eating ice cream.

"I know not to shoot you, dingbat. What about reloading? What if it jams?"

Cannon placed his hand over hers holding the gun. He guided her fingers along its shaft, then put her finger over the trigger. He took the other finger and placed it on the top of the gun. "A jam doesn't happen that often, and if that is the case, throw it away. Use this pipe as a second choice." He handed her the metal pipe from the backpack.

Cannon raised the gun in her hand to point away from them. He crouched behind her and showed her how to hold the gun, lining up himself against her arm. "You will probably cringe the first few times. Just stand with both hands like this." He guided her arms upward, placing one finger on the trigger, the other on the outside of the shaft. "You won't need to reload but try to focus on one shot at a time."

Cannon could feel her shaking as he moved with her. She wasn't used to holding a gun, so he knew she must be scared of what would happen to her. He let her go, and her arms were held in the air, focusing on an imaginary target.

"Ryver?"

"Yes?"

"You're going to be fine. I promise."

"Maybe you shouldn't promise those things."

Cannon sighed. "I mean it, though. The gun is just in case, but I will probably take them out quickly myself. I won't let anything happen to you."

Tears fell from her eyes. Cannon's heart ached

in his chest. "I don't want anything to happen to you either, Cannon. This can't be how it ends."

Cannon took her face in his hands. "It won't be." He wiped her tears, then kissed each eye individually.

Cannon didn't think their relationship could possibly pan out. Moreover, there was no part of the mission that said he needed to fall in love with her. But he did, and he wanted to be with her more than anything.

He could easily place her on the helicopter and just disappear. He put a hand on the back of his neck. No, his leash might be invisible, but it was strong.

A life without Ryver sounded like agony.

All thoughts were shattered when he heard the voices of the militia behind them – three, four, maybe five men – had emerged from the woods and were standing in the open field. One had spotted Cannon's giant frame.

Cannon's eyes went wide, and he looked at Ryver. His voice quivered as he whispered. "I'm going to shift, so I will leave my other gun here. It's already loaded too, so same deal."

Ryver pulled Cannon close for a deep kiss. He melted in her embrace.

"I believe in you," she whispered.

Cannon had a lump in his throat. He hadn't lost anything he loved so much in a long time. Cannon closed his eyes and allowed the intimate touch of his dragon come to life.

TWENTY-NINE

RYVER

"Stay here." Cannon had ordered Ryver. She held one gun in her hand, had the other by her side while the metal pipe was in the other hand. Her heart was pounding like a drum in her chest, but she knew she had to be on guard – she couldn't let her fear get the best of her.

Cannon stepped away, far enough so the men couldn't see her crouching. "I'm over here, you bastards."

One of the men laughed. Cannon took his shirt off.

The same man laughed loudly. "Oh, no need to show off! You will be dead soon enough."

Cannon closed his eyes after removing his pants. Ryver watched him fall into the deep meditative state that would allow him to shift quickly and efficiently.

The sun rose higher in the sky and highlighted the profound movement of man to monster. Ryver was honored that she could watch it happen, even in these circumstances.

Cannon opened his mouth so his razor-sharp teeth could find space in his mouth. It clicked and snapped. Scales grew out of his skin, and he heard the men beginning to yell. Ryver gasped, marveling as he changed. He had stepped outside behind the log and formed quickly. He roared at the men, who immediately began shooting at him.

He barreled toward them while Ryver sat in hiding. Cannon grabbed one of them with his teeth, instantly tearing them apart from the waist down. The man screamed in agony. He whipped his tail at another man, knocking him down and throwing the bullets high in the air. The third man managed to land a shot in the leg, penetrating his scales. He roared in pain. Ryver cringed, feeling his pain.

Cannon continued on fighting despite the attack. First, he kicked the man in the chin, his sharp nails piercing his neck and sending him to the ground in a flourish of blood. Cannon then took the other man, who had gotten up from the tail smack, between his teeth and pierced his flesh slowly.

The man screamed in pain, echoing across the field and into oblivion.

Ryver was paying too close attention to Cannon, worrying about him, to the point where she didn't notice a fifth man come up behind her.

The man grabbed her by the waist, pulling her back into him. Ryver was holding the gun and reminded herself of that when she became terrified. However, the man who had her didn't seem to be carrying any weapon at that point.

Ryver dug her nails into his hands, and the man yelped. She had time to spin around and strike him with the metal pipe Cannon had given her. A splash of blood flew out his mouth like red paint.

The man stumbled but did not fall. Ryver raised her hands to point the gun at him.

"Get the fuck away from us, or I will shoot!" Ryver bellowed.

The man was only wearing a ball cap. He wiped his face of the blood and smiled. "You're gonna have to shoot me, honey."

Hands shaking, Ryver placed her fingers on the

trigger. She was so close, but not fast enough. The man was too fast, leaping at her and smacking the gun from her grasp. Ryver watched the gun fall to the ground as the man jumped on top of her. He took a knife from his pocket and placed it at her neck.

"Shut up and come with us. You know you have no chance."

Ryver could hear skin being torn behind her. Cannon was still finishing off the men they had seen, but neither she nor Cannon realized there had been more watching. She panicked, fearing this man would kill her or successfully capture her. She pushed the knife away from her throat, tapping into the adrenaline that had saved her life in the past. She managed to get a hand free enough to punch the man in the balls. He dropped the knife, and he fell backward, clutching himself.

Ryver used that opportunity to leap onto the man. She had lost her gun but instead used the metal pipe against his throat. Her anger and love for Cannon allowed her strength to overcome his. He began choking, his legs shaking and eyes rolling back into his head.

"Yes! Take that motherfucker, take that..."

As the pipe pushed up against the man's vocal

cords, something hot blasted through Ryver's back. It made her lose her grip on the pipe, and she bolted up, then tumbled backward onto her butt. Something on fire had moved through her, and she was paralyzed with fear and pain. She was able to look down and see blood streaming from her lower back, and then she was finally able to compute what had happened to her; she had been shot.

Ryver craned her head back to see Cannon removing the head of one of the terrorists. Everyone had been killed, bodies thrown everywhere and torn to shreds. She was feeling dizzy but wanted to call out to him. He needed to know how her feelings before she died.

As she opened her mouth, the man in front of her had stood and had her by the throat. She could feel herself already giving into the release, the inability to breathe.

His grip got tighter, and before the world could fade away, Ryver watched as the man launched upward, screaming as Cannon grabbed him with a claw. Ryver turned as she fell onto her back to see the heroic sight of Cannon roaring into the man's face. The man was horrified, bellowing back at Cannon with spit and blood spewing from his mouth. Cannon ripped out his neck with a single tear of his mouth.

The man hung between his claws like a rag doll. Cannon tossed him aside like a piece of garbage.

Ryver smiled. Her hero, her savior. His colors burned orange, red, and golden in the sunrise light. She saw him shift in a blur, coming back to his human state to console her.

His face was still covered in blood, his leg bleeding from a bullet wound.

"Ryver, Ryver, can you hear me?"

She could hear him, but she could barely respond. Her wound was bottomless, and it continued to burn her insides. Her body was responding by slowly fading into the unconscious. But she didn't know if this meant she contained her energy or if she was dying.

"Cannon," Ryver whispered. Cannon was holding her in his arms and placed his wadded-up shirt over her wound. He put pressure on it, which made it hurt more.

"Yes," Cannon's eyes were wide and ferocious.

Ryver tugged at his neck. "Something is burning. Something is burning in me."

"I know, Ryver. You were shot. You're losing blood, but the helicopter should be here soon."

Ryver chattered, cold slipping through every part of her body. She tried to pull herself closer into his chest, but she could barely move. Cannon sensed this and moved her head to his chest, wrapping himself around her as much as he could.

"Your leg," Ryver's voice was husky and quiet. She realized Cannon had barely heard her before he reacted.

"I'm okay, sweetheart. Dragon scales are a bit like chainmail."

She reached for it. Cannon moved her hand back to his. He kissed each finger, tears swelling in the sun. "You don't have to worry about me. Just give yourself a break for once."

Ryver wanted to tell him she was in love with him. She wanted him to come back with her and live with her, to create a life together outside this madness. Even if she died, she wanted him to know she loved every single second they were together. So she reached out to touch his face.

"Cannon..."

"It's okay, Ryver. I promised it will be okay, and it will be."

She couldn't get the words out. It was the truth, but it hurt like hell.

"Cannon, I love yo..."

Ryver fell into darkness just as she heard the spinning of helicopter blades. It was as if her body was so filled with pain that it could no longer function – the pain from the bullet and the pain from her love. She didn't recall if she could get the words out fast enough.

THIRTY

CANNON

"Ryver? Ryver!" Cannon was screaming into the face of his love as the helicopter finally arrived. He was shaking Ryver, panicking as he had just lost the love of his life because of these fuckers. Finally, he heard it land behind him, and he lifted Ryver seamlessly. He ran to the chopper and handed her to the medic. Gus was there with the A.L.F.A. pilot.

"She's been shot!" Cannon yelled over the blades. "We need to get the fuck out of here! Now!"

As Cannon bellowed, a flurry of multiple terrorists emerged from the woods. They began firing at the chopper immediately. Cannon's rage built like an inferno.

"Go!" Cannon leaped into the helicopter, and it took off. He gripped the sides as the medic tended to Ryver, watching her face fade to pale white.

"What the fuck happened?" Gus yelled.

Cannon shook his head. "All these fuckers, that's what happened! We weren't briefed on them."

"We just learned of them when we scouted the area for your arrival. They were farther south in the Congo earlier," the agent replied. "We weren't worried about them at that point. I'm Parish Hamel, by the way."

"Thanks for coming to get us. But we need to get her to a hospital immediately. Are there more fighters in the area?"

"We didn't think these guys would be here," Gus answered. "They must've been on the move."

They weren't high in the sky when Cannon had a plan. He turned to Gus and placed a hand on his shoulder. "Don't wait for me. There may be more of them ahead, so I'm going to get rid of these and clear a path for you."

Gus was flabbergasted. "Cannon, we don't know what kind of ammo these guys have..."

"I don't give a shit! Just don't wait for me. Get her help immediately!"

Gus nodded, which permitted Cannon to sail out of the chopper. Cannon closed his eyes mid-jump, then shifted rapidly into his dragon. The dragon wanted blood, and it wanted revenge – it wanted to kill.

Cannon roared as he dropped down to the remaining terrorists. It had been some time since he used his fire abilities, and it wasn't always the best choice for neutralizing the enemy. But at that point, he didn't care. If Ryver was going to die, it was these sons of bitches' fault. He wanted to take them to hell with him.

Cannon breathed in through his large nostrils. His belly boiled with heat. Six to ten men shot at him, so he swirled to line them up. Cannon closed his eyes, his dragon lips bursting with blisters.

They were going to die a most painful death. He opened his mouth, seizing his stomach muscles to shoot fire that had stirred within him for what felt like thousands of years. It burned as it shot through his throat, but he didn't care. The men screamed and fled when they realized what was happening. They quickly caught fire and fell to the ground, their piercing cries music to Cannon's ears.

He turned a few times to ensure that the men were dead. They had ceased moving and were nothing more than fleshy pink bags of meat.

Cannon, tracing the path of the chopper, caught up, and they dropped low enough for him to jump in.

Cannon blinked heavily, then motioned in front of them.

Ryver was in his heart the entire time. The rage that coursed through him was directly linked with his love for her.

When the chopper landed on the hospital's roof, Cannon jumped out. Gus threw a blanket at his still-naked body. "Jesus, you still look good even when you're devastated."

Cannon ignored him as doctors and nurses rushed onto the roof. They placed Ryver on a gurney and ran her to the elevator. The agent reached out and touched his chest, a lame attempt to hold him back.

"She's in and out of consciousness. We have to wait for the doctors to do their thing."

Hamel watched him as he wrapped the

towel around himself. He still burned with anger despite having rid the area of those bastard humans.

"You feel for her, don't you? Jesus, what happened out there?" Gus said.

Cannon shot him a look. Initially, he was angry but then realized that his cohort had noticed an emotion in him he probably didn't see every day on missions such as these.

"I don't know. All I know is that I had no control over it," Cannon said, staring at the ground. The sun had risen, and he cast a giant shadow.

Before Gus could respond, three tall men dressed in all black approached them on the roof. Cannon already knew what it was going to be about before they spoke. "Cannon Dez?"

Cannon nodded. The man in sunglasses spoke again.

"General Nydia wants to debrief the mission immediately."

Gus burst out laughing. "Do you not see that the guy is naked and probably injured? Can we give him a second?"

The leader of the men looked down. Cannon also looked down, forgetting that he had been shot in the leg. It was an excellent way to get away from them and make a plan of escape. He knew that Nydia would revoke his privileges after nearly killing her daughter. His freedom would be taken away again.

But what about Ryver? He couldn't leave without seeing her.

"You're right. Let's get him to a nurse and retrieve him some clothes. Then we can debrief."

Cannon nodded, then a nurse immediately arrived. He thought pushing a wheelchair was unnecessary but sat in it anyway. He grunted, feeling his body finally relaxing after having been tense for hours.

The nurse rolled him into the elevator. Gus followed. The three men also entered the elevator and stood in front of him. The elevator doors closed, and Cannon and Gus exchanged a look. They were both shifters, so they could speak telepathically, but they didn't need it at that moment. They both knew there was some shit about to go down.

As the nurse rolled him out of the elevator, Cannon inquired. "Do you know where she is? My friend? What happened to her?"

The nurse continued pushing him. "She's

gone in for emergency surgery. We'll update you as soon as we know anything."

The nurse rolled him to an empty bed. Then, after one quick look at Cannon's size, she motioned to Gus. "Can you help me with him?"

Gus frowned but took Cannon by his armpits. The nurse took him by the legs and then set him down without mangling his leg. It didn't feel too bad to him – more like a stinging punch than a bullet wound – but he needed time to think.

"I'll get you something to wear after you're assessed," Gus said, then walked away. The three men were still standing over him, watching intently. Then, finally, the nurse went to draw the curtain. "Sorry, sirs, assessment is private."

None of the men objected when she pushed the curtain closed all the way. Cannon closed his eyes. He had to find a way out of here. Or perhaps a way to get what he wanted without being taken back to that fucking prison.

The nurse lifted the blanket covering the portion of his injured shin. She stared, then frowned intensely. Finally, she leaned in closer, hands leaning on her thighs. "Did you say you were shot?"

Cannon shrugged. Not every hospital was

aware of the defense abilities of shifters, and he didn't feel like explaining it to her. So he would play stupid for the time being.

"I thought I was, but maybe in the heat of the moment, it just slid past me."

"Hmm." She looked closer. "You see, there are some groves here that indicate penetration, but it's almost like the skin grew over."

Healing abilities. That's something else he also didn't want to talk about.

"I'm going to get the doctor, and I'll be right back." The nurse moved past the curtains, and Cannon saw a flicker of a look from one of the henchmen guarding him. When she left, he laid his head back, then sighed loudly. He just needed some fucking pants, and then he could find a way out of there.

THIRTY-ONE

RYVER

Ryver awakened to the sound of beeping. She opened her eyes and closed them, the light too bright to take. Her mind came to before her body did – she remembered being shot, trying to tell Cannon how much she loved him. She didn't know if she could even get the words out.

She saw something in her mind, something bloody and hurt. She could feel her heart shaking inside her. Memories rushed back to her like a flood.

Her heart filled with sadness, shocked, and incredibly aware of her situation.

A woman in blue scrubs was standing next

to her. She touched her arm when she panicked. "Miss? Miss Fernando? Everything is okay."

Ryver's chest heaved up and down. She was thinking about her father, about Cannon, about her injury. The nurse gripped her hand tightly.

"Just breathe in and breathe out. In through your nose, and out your mouth."

Ryver breathed in, then out. When she settled down, she held onto the nurse's hand. "What happened?" she asked.

The nurse rubbed her hand. "You were shot and had emergency surgery two days ago. I'm going to get the doctor to give you the complete update."

Ryver held onto her as the nurse tried to walk away. "Where is Cannon?"

The nurse frowned. "I'm sorry?"

"There was a man who was probably checked in with me, and he was shot. He's tall, red hair, very muscular."

The nurse thought for a second, then grinned. Cannon wasn't easy to miss. "We brought him in with you, yes. Let me just get the doctor to keep you up to date. Trust me, and it'll be okay."

That was the third or fourth time Ryver had heard that in the last few days. She wanted to believe it was true. But why wasn't Cannon there by her side?

The nurse left the room, and Ryver was briefly alone with her thoughts. She didn't feel any pain and noticed she was being pumped full of morphine. She tried to will the idea of whether or not she had told Cannon about her love for him. Indeed, if she had, he would either have been terrified by it or assured.

The doctor came into the room a few minutes later. She was a tall woman with short dark hair. Her eyes blazed with empathy as she entered the room.

"Hello, Ryver. I'm Angela Hendricks. I performed the surgery on you a couple days ago. How are you feeling?"

Ryver shook her head. "I feel fine. That isn't the problem."

"Well, let me explain everything to you before you start worrying." Her smile was wide. "So, as you know, two days ago, you were brought to us with a gunshot wound in your side. You were in and out of consciousness at the time, but we were able to put you under anesthesia for emergency surgery."

Dr. Hendricks pulled up the chair and sat.

She, too, placed a hand over Ryver's. It was warm and inviting. "We were able to pull out the bullet without causing any further damage. It appears to have gone through your left lower back and just missed your uterus."

The doctor paused, possibly waiting for Ryver to take in the information. Ryver was thankful, but the threat to her life, to her vital organs, seemed surreal within that moment. She sensed something pass between them, something crucial and life-changing.

"Miss Fernando, did you have any idea that you are pregnant?"

Ryver's heart shot up, and the machine began beeping rapidly. Her chest began heaving again, and Dr. Hendricks squeezed her hand again. "It's okay, Miss Fernando. The embryo just implanted a short time ago."

Ryver shook her head. She knew the father was Cannon as she hadn't slept with anyone in years. She was on birth control but hadn't had a pill since she was abducted.

Her emotions collided, feeling excitement, fear, and bewilderment. They now had a baby together, and she had no idea whether or not he even wanted to be in her life.

"Miss Fernando, the bullet just missed the fetus. So that is something that you don't have to worry about. Do you have any questions?"

Ryver stared into the distance. There was a window behind the doctor. One where she and Cannon could fly off and live together in some cabin in the mountains. And then they would have their baby.

But Cannon wasn't there, and she didn't know where to find him.

"I was curious where that man was, the one who was also brought in with me."

Dr. Hendricks nodded, then smiled. "Nurse Madison informed me that he was able to check out soon after. His injures were quite minimal."

Ryver wanted to burst out crying. He had left. He had just left her here, not knowing whether or not she was going to survive. Everything was a complete lie.

Dr. Hendricks, probably noticing the sense of betrayal and grief rising in her eyes, gave her another squeeze, then rose from her seat. "Please let the nurses know if you want to talk to any social services or psychiatrists. We can connect with you quite quickly. Again, I'm sorry about what happened to you. Just remember, whatever you want to do with this baby is your choice."

Dr. Hendricks left the room, leaving the echo of her words in Ryver's mind.

Without anyone around to judge her, Ryver burst into tears. She cried until her chest ached, then eventually stopped before her eyes stung too much. A part of her still wanted to hope he would return, that he needed to get everything lined up with her father.

But her brain also knew the truth. Maybe she was just a body to pass the time with. Someone to have sex with while he had the chance. He didn't want to go back to that prison, so why not get a few fucks in before heading off into the wilderness?

And now she had this baby to think about. She didn't know what she was going to do with it.

As she stared out the window, she decided that she would continue to make a difference in the world. She didn't need anyone else to help her do it. The baby would come with her, and she could take care of it on her terms.

The nurse returned to the room and brought her food. She smiled at her with sympathy, likely aware of what had transpired between her and the doctor.

"Nurse Madison?" Ryver asked.

"Yes?" Nurse Madison placed the tray in front of her and stood by her side.

Ryver sat up in her bed. "How much longer am I to stay here? I mean, if the surgery went well, am I able to check out whenever I want?"

The nurse shook her head. "It is recommended that you stay a few more days, but after then, the doctor will sign off on your release. It's good to get some rest, though." She patted Ryver's arm. It was a kindness she could not appreciate at the moment.

"Thank you." Ryver began spooning up her oatmeal, suddenly realizing how hungry she was. When the nurse left the room again, Ryver decided she wouldn't worry about Cannon right then. She didn't know whether or not she would tell him about the baby, if she even needed to. She didn't want him to feel obligated to be with her.

Her love for him continued to soar in her chest. Ryver wished she had told him earlier about her feelings, so she had known the disappointment in the jungle rather than in a hospital bed. But, instead, she scarfed down her breakfast and was starting to feel more confident about her decision.

Talented women who cared didn't need a man

to define them. Cannon wasn't going to take that away from her.

She was always going to hold him in her heart. He had cared for her, was gentle with her, and made her feel like she was important. His reasons for fleeing were confusing but might have been entirely practical. But whatever they were, they weren't hers anymore.

THIRTY-TWO

CANNON

When the nurse left Cannon behind the curtain, he breathed in a sigh of relief. But that relief lasted very briefly as the henchman standing watch received a call that made Cannon's heart stop.

"Yes, General, yes, we are on our way." The man in the sunglasses spoke over his phone. He pushed past the curtain and stared at his exposed leg.

"Um, a little privacy here?" Cannon said with a sarcastic tone.

"The general wants to see you immediately. She's checked in at the hotel across the street. How injured are you?"

Within the same instant that the henchman

was questioning Cannon, a male doctor passed through the curtains. He looked at the henchman, then back at Cannon. "Hi, there, I'm Dr. Mbabazi. I was told you were just brought in, and you believed you were shot?"

Cannon smiled. "Merely grazed, I think. But, of course, you never know what is happening in the heat of battle."

Dr. Mbabazi bent over to examine the wound. By that point, it had almost healed completely, appearing more like a scrape on the playground than anything close to a gunshot wound. The doctor turned to the nurse. "Stitch him up a bit, and then he can be on his way." He left without another word, giving the men dressed in all black a narrow-eyed look.

"If you could stand behind the curtain, I'll have him finished in no time, gentlemen." The nurse gathered the henchman away from Cannon, pulling the curtain back. She stitched him up quickly, which was probably unnecessary. She bandaged him, then gave him a prescription for pain medication. Cannon held the paper between his fingers.

"So I'm good to go then?"

The nurse nodded and pulled back the

curtain. The henchmen were ready to go. They hauled him to his feet with the bed sheet wrapped around him. Cannon considered breaking off from them and fleeing, but then he wouldn't be able to return to find Ryver. She might think he had abandoned her. Those were the last thoughts he wanted to go through her mind.

So he went along with them, trying to plan if things were to go wrong. He wasn't sure what the general wanted from him besides an actual briefing. Things were rarely how they seemed with her.

The men took Cannon to the hotel, still wrapped in the blanket. They gave him clothes to change into while they were in the car. He put them on after they parked while the henchmen simply waited outside. That was another excellent opportunity to flee, but he knew he could not take it.

The men sequestered Cannon through the lobby and into the elevator. Cannon stood almost a foot taller than them, something he noticed as they stood in the lift in silence. He could easily take them out, right then and there, just with a few swings of his elbows. But he closed his eyes and thought of Ryver – only Ryver.

They took Cannon to a room down the hall,

knocking on the door twice. "Enter," a familiar voice replied. Nydia. Cannon heaved a big sigh and entered the room.

Nydia was sitting on the couch with a glass of wine perched between two fingers. She was sleek in an all-black suit, her blond hair looking recently straightened from its natural curls. She was mid-sip when he caught her eye. "Cannon Dez, thank God, you've made it back to us."

"There wasn't ever any other option."

Cannon was made to sit in front of her. Her eyes were blazing, and he wasn't sure if it was from rage, satisfaction, or simply just a look of power. She smiled at him, all teeth, then placed the glass of wine on the coffee table. "It looks like you got more than you bargained for."

Cannon tried not to gulp. Instead, he stared at Nydia, indifferent.

Nydia burst into a fit of laughter. The other men in the room looked around, startled. "I know you fucked my daughter, so don't look so confused."

This time Cannon did swallow. How did she know so soon? Wait, she knew Ryver was her daughter?

Her brows rose with her grin. "What? You

didn't think I knew who I sent you after? I was relieved to see her alive when she came out of surgery. She was on so many drugs, but I knew that part of her babbling to the nurses was true. She said she's in love with you."

Cannon could feel his heart swelling. He was so tired but relieved that she thought the same. His fear dissipated like ice in the sun.

Nydia continued to stare at him. She sighed. "You completed the mission, Cannon, all without failure, and a shit load of bumps in the road. Congratulations."

Without warning, there was a sucking motion at the back of his neck. Then, a high-pitched noise confirmed that it was the device that removed his implant from the prison. Now he had been released of the suicide bug.

Cannon rubbed the back of his neck, looking around at the henchman.

"But doing a good job comes with strings, Cannon," Nydia continued. "I'm going to promote you to the commander of the elite force I told you about."

Cannon was joyous over having his complete shifter. Nydia picked up her glass of wine, sipping between words. "You won't be alone anymore, Cannon, and I'm going to remove the bug from Bolt next."

Cannon perked up. Bolt was a longtime friend who shifted into tiger form. Working with him would be easy because trust was something they'd formed very early in their relationship. Working and helping other shifters excited Cannon – but he also wanted a life with Ryver.

"If you don't mind me saying," Cannon interjected. "I... I want to see your daughter. I appreciate the promotion, but I, I want to be with her."

Nydia swirled the wine between her fingers. "You mean you love her too?"

Tears stung his eyes. He nodded. "She came out of surgery, okay?"

Nydia nodded. "You successfully saved her. But, unfortunately, she is going to be out a few days to recover, and you must wait for the attention you created in the hospital to die down."

Cannon frowned. Nydia finished off her glass and placed it down with a clink. "The nurse knew you were a shifter. We can't have them knowing that you were part of a mission – the elite force is still very much under the radar."

Cannon nodded, understanding. But he still

needed to see Ryver. "I want her to know how I feel, General. She can't think I just left."

Nydia stood and made her way toward the door. "You have time, Cannon. She isn't going anywhere for a few days. I reserved this room for you to wait in. Go in two days to see her."

The henchmen followed behind her, and her hand was on the handle as she turned to Cannon, flashing her bright blue eyes. "And Cannon?"

Cannon stood.

She smiled. "Thank you."

Cannon smiled back. "You should talk to her. She thinks you're dead, you know."

She dropped her chin to her chest. "Yes, that was the story I told her father to tell her when she was old enough."

"Why?" he asked, baffled.

She sighed. "I've made mistakes, Cannon. Just like everyone else. I was young and pregnant and determined to be someone. I thought a family would hold me back."

"You should tell her."

She shook her head. "No, I don't want her to know who I've become. But there hasn't been a day I haven't thought of her. Maybe someday when my past no longer haunts me. Someday when I'm no longer the person I am."

With that, she walked out. He watched the door close, not sure what the right thing to do was. Maybe if she ever retired, he would introduce them. Then again, maybe she wasn't worthy of Ryver.

Cannon waited two full days to return to the hospital. He spent them bathing, pacing, drinking, and barely sleeping a wink. He kept the curtains open to watch the front entry and exit if Ryver chose to depart early. He didn't want to betray Nydia's confidence. Afterall, she'd given him his freedom back.

Cannon made his way to the hospital in the evening of the second day. He tried to make himself as inconspicuous as possible, but he was a tall man with red hair – that was difficult to hide. When he inquired about her room, the hospital told him she had checked out.

"When?" he asked, trying not to rage.

"A few minutes ago." The nurse couldn't tell him exactly where she had gone, but her head had motioned toward the exit, and Cannon used his senses. He followed her scent, those beautiful waterlilies and cinnamon.

"Ryver! Ryver, wait!"

She held two large bags and was about to climb into a cab. She turned to him, and her look ran cold. "Cannon, please don't do this."

Cannon ran toward her. "Ryver, I'm sorry, I had to stay away. They don't know about the program and your..." He'd almost said *mother*.

"I don't need to hear this, Cannon."

"No, please listen to me."

He took her by the forearms. He looked deeply in her crystal eyes – so much like her mother's. "I'm in love with you, Ryver. I want you to marry me."

Ryver's eyes widened, and she dropped her bags. "You do?"

Cannon nodded. "I do."

Ryver's eyes swelled with tears. She fell into his arms and began sobbing. "I love you too, Cannon, so much. Why did you leave me alone?"

"I'm sorry, love." He hugged her harder. "It was out of my hands. But I'll never leave you alone like that again."

THIRTY-THREE

RYVER

Ryver told Cannon about her pregnancy when they were on the plane back to the States. Cannon hugged and kissed her until her mouth and chest hurt from laughing. She was beyond delighted by his happiness.

"I never thought I would find this Ryver," Cannon said while he held her.

"Me either, darling, me either," Ryver whispered into his chest, finally calming, finally feeling safe in his arms again. There was no one left to chase them down, no more reservations required for their love to flourish.

Finally, outside her apartment building, Ryver took Cannon by the hand into her home. It was neat since she hadn't been there in months. She flicked the light on, and Cannon awed at it for a moment. All of the appliances were metallic and new, the furniture plushy and modern. "Wow, so these are the swanky duds you get when you're a doctor."

Ryver almost had to jump to grab Cannon by the face and pull his down to hers. Their mouths collided, and they kissed passionately. Cannon wrapped his arms around her waist and lifted her onto the kitchen counter. She giggled and ran her hands through his hair.

"This seems more even." Cannon was grinning widely. His face looked so bright in her kitchen. All of the mud and dirt from the jungle had faded, and that gloss of fear. His eyes were shining at her, and she couldn't help but blush. She pushed his hair out of his face and kissed his forehead.

"You want this baby, Cannon?"

Cannon frowned. "More than anything. It's true that I never thought this would happen to me, nor that I would want it. But I want it with you. So you don't have to worry about that anymore. I'm here."

He tilted her chin toward him, their lips

hovering closely over one another's. She breathed into him, and him into her. She smiled. "I love you so much, Cannon. I hope you know that."

"I do. And I love you beyond any words spoken." They plunged into one another relentlessly. Ryver ran her fingers through Cannon's thick locks and over his back while Cannon gripped her hips and squeezed her ass. They were trying to meld into one another, evaporate into their bodies, and ultimately become one.

Ryver wanted to feel him all over her. She wanted to feel his skin, his mouth, his fingers, his entire body, without fear of abandonment, fear of judgment, or of capture. She pulled at his T-shirt and began lifting it over his head. She immediately relished in his warm body, pressing her face into his neck and breathing in his intoxicating scent.

While she did this, Cannon had reached behind her and unclipped her bra in one swift motion. Ryver pulled away to display faux shock. "Wow, someone is handy!"

Cannon chuckled. "I figured you want to get right down to business." Their mouths met and danced once more. Cannon lifted her shirt, along with her bra, over her head and tossed it onto the linoleum beneath them. He stood back for a moment, admiring her body, and Ryver blushed, instinctively trying to cover herself. Cannon then took her by the wrists.

"Don't you dare, missy. I'm trying to admire this piece of art."

"You can do that better with your hands." Ryver took his hands and placed them over her breasts. She moaned at his touch, her nipples already erect. He sighed for a long time. Ryver reached down and unzipped his pants. "Now I want to touch."

He was hard in his underwear. She couldn't believe how big he was and how quickly he got an erection. She loved the feel of him, even through clothing.

Cannon removed his hands from her breasts for a moment to take off his pants. He stood there, spectacularly hard under the fluorescent lights, dazzlingly thick and veiny. She pulled him in again to kiss him, feeling his cock rubbing against her leg.

He pulled away and smiled. "Let me take you to the bedroom."

She nodded, and he swiftly whipped her upward in a gentle cradle. He removed her pants and panties in a single movement, leaving her in awe at his skills once more. He then moved into the bedroom, where he placed her softly on the bed. His eyes continued to shine in the darkness. He turned on the bedside lamp, then climbed on top of her. He watched her for a moment without moving, merely hovering over her body.

"What are you looking at, handsome?"

She touched his face, running a single finger down from his forehead to his lips. He kissed it, then lowered himself. She could feel his hardness pressing into her leg. She wanted him so badly, her body ached. "Cannon, I need you."

"I know, Ryver, and I need you too. I want this forever, you know. I want you to know that."

Ryver kissed him hard, and they made out for some time, naked bodies rocking against each other like the waves against the shore. Eventually, he sat up and slowly guided himself inside her. She arched her back at the sensation, reeling in the way he managed to touch every corner of her insides. Cannon kissed and nibbled at her neck. Finally, he moved inside her, and she moved with him.

Their breaths became quickly succinct, as did their bodies. Their soft crashing together and wordless exchange of passion brought them into a transcendent point of connection, one that not any song, piece of poetry, or sentiment could capture. It was love, and love needed not a single word.

They moved together, entirely at ease and in the moment. Ryver could feel her arousal quickly heightening, getting to the point of utter release. Her climaxes would be different from then on. Instead of being out of desperation, they would thrive and enrich every interaction. Cannon was no student to pleasure, and it was something she could always guarantee within their relationship.

The pair moved faster, slightly rocking the headboard against the wall. Cannon placed his hands around her neck and pushed harder inside her. Ryver loved it and begged for more with the movement of her hips. She wrapped her hands around his shoulders and pulled him closer. He breathed into her ear as she did into his. She told him how much she loved him, and he told her. She wanted him to cum inside her, but he wanted her to cum first.

They moaned together in their selfless exclamation of love. Ryver reached her climax with extraordinary intensity – she swore she almost wept at the height of the minute-long orgasm. She cried out his name into his ear, biting it slightly as her muscles seized, then relaxed into the dopamine rush. Cannon came soon after, spilling himself inside her, collapsing on top of her, breathing his warm breath. He huffed and growled, nibbling at her neck.

"Oh, Cannon."

"Ryver, you're incredible. I wish I could tell you how incredible you are."

Ryver smiled, kissing his sweaty shoulder. "You can always try, and I will listen."

Cannon rolled off of her and lay beside her, stroking her arm while his breathing became shallower. "And that I will do."

She turned to him, stroking his face. "Do you think our child will get shifting abilities?"

Cannon scrunched his face together. Maybe. He hadn't thought of that. "It's possible. Maybe, maybe not."

"I don't care. Either way, Cannon, we will love them." Ryver kissed him and settled onto his chest. His heart was pounding, and she loved the serenade.

"It would be interesting to teach someone so young about it. I've never met a young shifter," Cannon said, staring up at the ceiling.

Ryver nodded against him.

"Either way, though," Cannon said as he

stroked her hair. "They're going to have some badass fucking parents."

Ryver giggled. "Can you imagine telling them how we met, though?"

Cannon's face turned grim. "Yeah, let's skip the part about how many times we fucked in the forest."

Ryver sat up, smiling. "Or how you gave me my first experience of multiple orgasms."

Cannon roared with laughter. "Oh, definitely skipping that detail."

They laughed and talked deep into the night. No longer fleeing for their lives or fearing not having enough food for the approaching day or about how many different kinds of militia were going to take them out. They only needed to think about each other and their path. They would walk side-by-side. A shifter and a human soaring across the world into eternity.

THIRTY-FOUR

RYVER

Ryver knew Cannon loved her because a few days after their return home in the United States, he took her on the date she had been craving. He had a slew of movies ready for her to choose from, as well as the multitude of ice cream flavors laid out on the kitchen table, with an assortment of toppings.

"Because you never actually got to tell me what your favorite was..." Cannon said, motioning toward the impressive display.

Ryver giggled. "I love every kind of ice cream, don't you worry." She kissed him and began selecting her choice. She took a scoop of everything, indulging in chocolate, vanilla, mint, raspberry ripple, and caramel. Cannon's eyes went wide as she brought her bowl out to the couch. "Jesus Christ, someone is having a sugar rush tonight."

She smiled and elbowed him. "That's what the movies are for!"

They took a few moments to select a romantic comedy, an action thriller, and a horror film. All day, they watched movies and laughed together, letting the rain fall outside their love nest.

In between films, they wondered if they should get something to eat. "You mean dinner? I thought ice cream was dinner." Cannon prodded at her.

Ryver was lying on the couch, clutching her stomach. "I'm a terrible cook. You're going to have to be the one to take on that job because I never learned."

Cannon exaggerated a frown. "But what about your womanly duties?"

Ryver reached over and lightly slapped his arm. He recoiled, laughing.

"Well, what about your manly duties?"

Cannon shook his head in between bites of vanilla ice cream. "That's your job now. You'll learn to shoot, and I'll learn to cook."

Ryver grinned, then sat up. "I really could use a few lessons about that."

Cannon nodded. "It's a good skill to have in general."

Ryver giggled louder. Cannon furrowed his brows. "What?"

"You've got something there." Ryver touched her lip.

"Here?" He touched his face, intentionally in the wrong spot.

"No, here, you idiot!" Ryver reached out and tried poking at Cannon's face, but he blocked it. In the middle of their tussle, Cannon heard a knock at the door. He froze for a moment, holding Ryver's arms away from her.

"Who could that be?" Ryver asked, getting up to answer her door. She wiped her face and looked through the peephole. On the other side of the door stood a stern-looking older blonde with straight short hair she'd never seen before. She opened the door and gave her best impression of friendliness. "Hi, can I help you?"

Cannon was suddenly beside her. The woman nodded at her the way a sergeant nods at their cadets.

"I'm here to speak with Cannon."

Cannon leaned against the door frame with his arms crossed. "You can say anything in front of her. We're going to be husband and wife soon."

The woman's eyes widened. Ryver wanted to ask who this lady was, but the tension worried her. Was he in some kind of trouble? The female placed her hands behind her back and looked at them down her nose. She seemed like such a bitch.

"I'm happy for you both." Her expression was plain and did not align with her words. "Cannon, I want to remind you that, despite eloping with your target acquisition, you are still on-call for a mission as the commander at any point. I hope you can respect our deal." She met his gaze and held it. "People's freedoms depends on it."

Cannon nodded. "I'm committed to both my family and the team. I made a promise. You have my word on that."

For the first time within that interaction, the lady smiled. Suddenly, the stranger looked familiar. "I'm sorry," Ryver said, "Have we met before?"

"Your father is in the military. There is always a possibility." The older lady left without another word. Cannon and Ryver looked at each other. She couldn't read his expression. Then it dawned on her.

"Oh, shit. *That* was the general?" she whisper-yelled. She wanted to give the woman a piece of her mind, but she was gone. Cannon grabbed her arm and pulled her into a kiss that curled her toes. She wondered if he was trying to distract her from something.

CANNON BOUGHT Ryver a proper ring two weeks later. It was large and shined in the bedroom's light. She cried when he put it on her finger, officially getting down on one knee.

"I'm assuming you will marry me?" Cannon grinned.

Ryver laughed through tears and pushed him down, climbing on top of him and making love deep into the night.

Two months later, Cannon and Ryver wed in a private ceremony in the countryside. Cannon invited the few shifter friends who weren't in prison, most of them military, while Ryver invited a handful of friends and family and her father. The ceremony took place outside on a sunny day – nothing but blue skies above them.

They exchanged vows while holding hands

and staring into each other's eyes. Cannon towered over Ryver and the minister, but she didn't mind looking up into his stunning ocean-blue eyes. She had never seen him so happy and couldn't believe she was the cause of it.

"I will soar to the highest heights with you, for you are my home, and wherever we shall go, home is you." Cannon finished his vows, wiping a tear from his eye.

"You're the sun to my sky, the moon to my night, the songbird at dawn. You are my everything, Cannon." They kissed, and their friends frenzied in claps behind them. When they walked down the aisle, Ryver felt like she had just sprouted wings herself.

The reception took place in a small bar in town. They set up the area with adorning lights that streamed into the yard and tiny pictures of the couple strewn about in decorative lines hanging over each table. Ryver wasn't drinking, of course, but she held a glass of champagne in one hand anyway. She looked up at her husband, who was holding her hand and watching the guests mingle. Her father, who had already given them his blessing was actively interacting with some family members. He stopped by and kissed Ryver on the cheek and shook Cannon's hand.

"Welcome to the family, son."

Those were the best words her father could have ever said in front of her.

She tapped Cannon's shoulder. "I think I want to do it now."

Cannon looked down at her, smiling. "You can do it whenever you want, wife. Let's get some people inside first." Cannon kissed her, and they lingered for a moment. She couldn't believe she had got to call this man her husband. For a moment, Cannon left to gather guests back inside so Ryver could make her announcement. When he returned, he stood at her side.

Ryver picked up a spoon and clinked it against the glass. Then, she asked the bartender to turn off the music and rang the glass louder. Eventually, everyone hushed and turned their attention to the beaming couple. Her father winked at her, already knowing her announcement.

"Thank you so much for everyone who came today. I know it was short notice, but well, we never actually planned on meeting!"

The crowd laughed together. Ryver twirled

a glass in her fingers and instinctively rubbed her stomach. Then, someone in the group gasped – one of her friends from medical school.

"There was something else that we didn't plan either, and that was what we wanted to share with you all before the night comes to an end." She turned to look at Cannon, whose face glowed with pride. Then, she turned back to the crowd. "We're pregnant!"

The crowd roared with applause and laughter. "So that's why I've been holding onto this glass all night instead of drinking it!"

Everyone laughed again, then began gathering around her. Cannon stepped so her friends and family can hug her and congratulate her. She sensed him watching her, his warm love casting a layer over her entire being.

She reached out for him, pulling him back in close. Friends and family congratulated them both. Ryver couldn't believe how quickly everyone was approving of them, how happy they were for the new life they were creating together. She wished her mother could have been there, could've seen how happy she was, could've met her grandchild. Still, she met her dad's smile and blew him a kiss. She had him. She'd always have him.

Ryver didn't want that to spoil the moment. So she held tightly onto Cannon's hand as everyone lined up to congratulate them on their fortune. After a myriad of hugs and kisses, Ryver overflowed with emotions.

Cannon grinned down at her, sweeping her against him into a hug. "You ready to head out to the airport? Our ride to Portugal awaits, my love."

Ryver laid her head on Cannon's chest. "Let's just stay away from any jungles, okay?"

AS RYVER LEFT the reception area to change into traveling clothes, Cannon made a beeline for the guest he saw arrive a short time ago. The woman had snuck in unbeknownst to his bride.

Cannon kept his voice calm. "General, I wondered if you would make an appearance at your daughter's wedding."

Anderson, dressed in a navy-blue power suit, raised a brow at him.

"Of course," she replied, "I've yet to miss any of my daughter's big life events."

That surprised him. He'd thought that this

career-driven officer had no emotional attachments to the family she rejected so long ago.

"Don't look so shocked, Cannon. I know you would rather see me dead than as your mother-in-law."

His knees nearly gave way with that knowledge suddenly thrust upon him. Nydia let out a loud laugh he'd never heard from the woman.

He quickly regained his lost composure. "Then as the person who loves your daughter and wants her happiness, you know I have to tell her about you. I can't keep this up. I owe her the truth and so do you. How can I keep such a secret from her? It's been killing me having to hide this. It's not right."

She frowned. "No, Cannon. This isn't your story to tell. You'll only hurt her more if you get involved between us. Do you want that?"

Of course, he didn't. But he couldn't just let this all be swept under the rug, either. He asked, "Why did you come by her apartment after we got back from Uganda? I'm sure it wasn't only to remind me of my obligation."

The general sighed. "It wasn't. I guess I wanted to see if you'd said anything about me to her."

"That was the perfect time—"

"No, Cannon," she growled. "As I said before, when the time is right, I will try to make up for all I've done. But not until then." The general clasped her hands behind her, straightening her back, and shifted into the hard-ass female soldier he knew her as. "Might I remind you, Cannon, that you are still under my command and I have quite a lot of power in the ranks. It is your duty to follow orders or face the consequences. Don't do anything that would jeopardize my daughter's happiness. That includes turning her life upside down just before having a baby."

Ah fuck. They were about to bring a new life into the world. What kind of stress and anguish would he throw on Ryver if he delved into forcing a relationship between the women right now? Dammit, dammit, dammit. He was between a rock and a hard place. But he refused to keep this from the woman he loved.

"I'll make a deal with you, General," he said. "She's my mate. There are to be no lies or hidden truths between us. I'll let you tell your story to Ryver when you're ready if you give me your word that the day will come soon. I won't wait much longer. It's not right to keep this from her."

"You're right. It's not, but I have my reasons, Cannon." Her brows raised as she glanced across the crowded room. He followed her line of sight to see his beautiful Ryver had returned from changing. "Do your damnedest to keep her safe and happy, Cannon." With that, she about-faced and hurried out the door.

He stood and watched her leave wondering if he'd done the right thing. Ryver wrapped herself around him. "Hey, what's the long face for?"

He smiled and kissed the top of her head. "Because I'm having to wait to get you all to myself."

She poked him in the stomach. "Don't be silly. We have all the honeymoon to our lonesomes."

He wrapped his arm around her shoulders and walked her toward the front of the room to say their good-byes before leaving. "You're right. Do me a favor," he said, "sometime later, ask me about the prison warden. I remember hearing about some good things she did during her military career."

Ryver stopped in her tracks. "Wait, is this the same General Anderson you hate?"

He shrugged. "I may have been a little harsh on her at the time. You never know what someone has gone through until you hear their story, you know?"

He gave her a huge smile knowing that, one way or the other, he'd make sure the woman he loved was treated like the incredible woman she was. "Now, let's go to Portugal."

The End...for now

ABOUT THE AUTHOR

New York Times and USA Today Bestselling Author

Hi! I'm Milly Taiden. I love to write sexy stories featuring fun, sassy heroines with curves and growly alpha males with fur. My books are a great way to satisfy your craving for paranormal romance with action, humor, suspense and happily ever afters.

I live in Florida with my hubby, our son, and our fur babies: Speedy, Stormy and Teddy. I have a serious addiction to chocolate and cake.

I love to meet new readers, so come sign up for my newsletter and check out my Facebook page. We always have lots of fun stuff going on there.

SIGN UP FOR MILLY'S NEWSLETTER FOR LATEST NEWS!

http://eepurl.com/pt9q1

Find out more about Milly here:

www.millytaiden.com

milly@millytaiden.com

ALSO BY MILLY TAIDEN

Find out more about Milly Taiden here:

Email: millytaiden@gmail.com

Website: http://www.millytaiden.com

Facebook: http://www.facebook.com/millytaidenpage

Twitter: https://www.twitter.com/millytaiden

You can find a complete list of all my books by series and reading order at my website: millytaiden.com

Printed in Great Britain
by Amazon

79875025R00188